MEETING ON THE STEPS TO HADES

MEETING ON THE STEPS TO HADES

a novel by

Ron Savage

NEW PULP PRESS

Published by New Pulp Press, LLC, 926 Truman Avenue, Key West, Florida 33040, USA.

For information contact:
Publisher@NewPulpPress.com

ISBN-13: 978-1945734229 (New Pulp Press)
ISBN-10: 1945734221

Printed in the United States of America
Visit us on the web at www.newpulppress.com

To my Janny, for her love
and kindnesses

Underneath my lids another eye has opened
it looks nakedly
at the light

that soaks in from the world of pain
even when I sleep

Steadily it regards
everything I am going through

and more

it sees the clubs and the rifle-butts
rising and falling
it sees

detail not on TV

From *The Prison House*

-- Adrienne Rich

MEETING ON THE STEPS TO HADES

1

August, 2013
Madrid, Spain

Mrs. Grendel's new job

SHE WALKED THROUGH the Casa de Campo to the area where the adolescent boys worked their scarlet capes and measured steps. Little bullfighters. Future bleeders. These were the apprentice *toreros* of the Escuela Taurina de Madrid. This had impressed Liesbet Grendel enough to purchase her own cape, something in white cotton. She'd worn capes in the past, yes, even white ones, but nothing so glamorous. It draped across her shoulders and had a silver hook and chain at the collar. "White reflects sunlight, you know. Keeps the body cool in the summer." She would say that to people who gave her the "So What Are You Supposed to be?" look. The tourist crowd, mainly – Mr. and Mrs. *Puto-Puta*. Waddlers too ass fat for their shorts. *Have they taken an inventory of themselves lately?* Mrs. Grendel thought. *What does it take to understand the value of*

self-improvement? Obesity wasn't the only issue, either. Every day was laundry day for the *Puto-Putas*. They seemed to dress in whatever was left at the bottom of their bureau drawer. Clothing you'd wear if you had absolutely nothing else to wear. Maroon stretch pants and a chartreuse t-shirt, whatever. You know the type, out of it but still f-ing smug. This never happened with Spaniards. Oh Spaniards have their faults. Who doesn't? But

they under*stand* capes. Spain has always appreciated the glamour and drama of the cape.

Last week Mrs. Grendel had gone to El Corte Ingles, an enormous tan brick department store in central Madrid. Lots of glass and oddly beautiful, the upper part resembled the tiered decks of a cruise ship, the lower part a sand dune.

"How *ele*gant, Senora," the salesman had told her. "The cape, it's always a daring touch, yes?" The man had slicked back dark hair and a thin mustache that ended at the corners of his mouth. His slender hands were pressed together as he talked, his English accented only slightly. "If you'll forgive a personal observation, the senora wears it so perfectly."

"You don't think it's too much?"

"On *you*? Not at all."

Mrs. Grendel studied herself in the full-length mirror.

Yes, definitely her. It allowed a girl have her clever secrets, didn't it? *The things one could hide!* Men loved their mystery women. Look at Greta Garbo, rest her soul. Or the movie *Laura* where Dana Andrews puts together a dead Gene Tierney's life and falls in love with her.

Capes conceal their owners. Mrs. Grendel's compact presence, the muscular arms and legs, her obsession with free weights and exercise, the cape hid it all. She could have been in her late-forties or early fifties; on a particularly bad day, maybe sixty-one or two. But the day would have to be pretty f-ing bad. Suicidally bad. Now there were days she would, say, *test* herself. Go into iffy neighborhoods with a plump handbag and a fragile attitude. *Come on, sweetmeats, rob me. Try it. Here kitty, kitties.* Mrs. Grendel did not think of this as suicidal. She thought of it as training. Training with faggy bullies who wanted it in the butt so bad they'd spend their time smacking around gays and old folks. *Kissy, kissy, bitch boys.* Bed-Stuy, Brooklyn. East LA. Humbolt Park, Chicago. She'd trained in each of them – more, really, cities in other countries, many cities. Boris de Boulonge Park in Paris. Ghitorni Metro Station in Delhi. The West End in London. *Hey here I am, an old lady with a handbag. Come and get me, hurry, hurry.*

Mrs. Grendel's training had no end. Would a cellist quit her practice? Would a fighter go into the ring and not first spar with a partner? She was a student who refused summers by the pool, her studies never finished, her last test never given, her graduation never less than retirement or death – if there was such a thing as death, as The End, The Glorious Finale. And couldn't she make the most of that?

Be still my heart.

Today beneath Mrs. Grendel's cape was a narrow leather sheath strapped to her left forearm. Inside the sheath was a metal pick. She had made the pick many years ago, perhaps close to...*why bother to guess, the years go on* – a twelve-inch blade rounded by a lathe and ground very thin and very sharp. On one end of the pick was a pearl handle with grooves that matched her fingers.

THEY WERE HAVING drinks after work, Annie Silva and her new friend Fr. Rafa. No, that wasn't it. That sounded *far* too chummy – not a friend, exactly, more a co-worker who had insisted. "It will do you good," he'd said. *Fine, a drink is a drink.* Now the friar watched her but kept silent. Annie felt self-conscious.

Maybe she wasn't Spanish enough for him. Too curly-haired, too chunky, too much of a dark-eyed

Semitic, perhaps even too American, who can figure other people.

Shit. Who can figure men.

She and the friar sat under thickly leafed oaks at a café table in the Plaza de Santa Ana. The day had left the air warm and sticky, the sky threaded pink from the last of the sun. This particular café served excellent tapas and wine – lovely tapas, *calamares fritos, jamon Serrano, tortilla a la Española.* Annie had ordered a glass of red, the crianza, and an order of the salt-cured ham. Fr. Rafa was not a tapas man nor a wine man, either. He was having what he usually had, his evening martini with two olives – vodka of course, not gin, *never* gin – and the vodka should be Girona made in the city of the same name, a few miles northeast of Barcelona. The vodka should also be cold enough to numb the back of the throat.

"I was told you began preparing for this job months ago," Fr. Rafa said.

"A year and two months, I think. At least two."

"– Just to restore a painting. I'm stunned, really."

Annie had met Rafa last week at the Museo del Prado. She'd been commissioned to work in the museum's conservation studio on the painting *Meeting on the Steps to Hades* by Luc Grendel, a 16th century Flemish artist and considered the favorite among the three Hieronymus Bosch protégées. The museum had assigned Fr. Rafa to discuss the painting's history and symbolism with her.

"I'm here to give you a sense of things," he had said. "After all, a picture is more than the stroke of a brush. Wouldn't you agree?"

"I'm a conservator, father."

"A very good one, I'm sure."

The Prado had followed her instructions with the sort of detail and skill that went beyond what she'd requested – over two hundred high definition slides. Specific angles of where the painting would be displayed, different lighting possibilities, the museum's detail was remarkable. The slides were sent to her home in Brentwood, California. Annie then proceeded to reconstruct the painting from its linen on poplar surface to the colors used by Flemish artists of that time. Both the pigments and the glue for the linen were made from animal fat and tissue. Horses, goats, pigs, whatever had been available. For this Annie had gone to a small slaughter house in Stockton.

The easiest part was painting the *Meeting on the Steps to Hades*. Though she'd never say it out loud, Annie thought her version of the painting was better than the one done by Grendel. From arranging the photos, gather supplies and finally putting brush on linen, the painting took two months and five days to complete. She didn't go through this for every job, thank God. Yes, she did want to get a feel for the artist, how he had gone about his work, the problems that he'd faced. But there was also a sensible part to it. If the Prado liked her work, there would be more trips to Madrid, more jobs to do.

LIESBET GRENDEL WAS sitting on a wood bench, still in the Casa de Campo, near a cluster of pines and across from the wide sandy area where the apprentice *toreros* of the Escuela Taurina de Madrid practiced with their scarlet capes. The early night sky was clear and there were some stars and a cut of white moon. Though the air remained humid from the day, the white cotton cape covered her arms.

Only one boy remained now.

He made graceful turns under the yellow lamplight, his cape following him in a quiet flutter, his slender body straight and arced slightly at the small of the back. Mrs. Grendel wondered if the boy had ever imagined a crowd shouting his name, cheering him on – this little bullfighter, this *torero*. She suspected that was so. He doubtlessly pictured himself dressed in his *traje de luces*, walking up to the President's Box, bowing before a beautiful senorita the way the actor Robert Evans did in *The Sun Also Rises*.

Don't they all see themselves doing that?

The Casa de Campo also had its disreputable side. Prostitutes wandered the park at night and many men strolled the walkways looking for prostitutes. There is a Spanish saying, "No sucede lo que sucede en la oscuridad." *What happens in the dark does not happen*. Mrs. Grendel thought this was amusing, how most cultures have a place to do things people want to do without other people knowing they are doing them. In Madrid the Casa de Campo was such a place, respectable by day and contemptuous by night.

It felt good, returning to this city. A person could disappear in Madrid and never be missed. Mrs. Grendel had been here numerous times, dozens, more. She'd lost count. There were places large enough to kill who needed killing and – with planning, one had to have a plan – leave before the penalties caught up with you. Madrid was like that. Cairo, Mexico City, Mumbai, Beijing were like that, too.

Then Ms. Grendel recalled a recent conversation.

"She is in Madrid," the fat man had told her.

"A lovely city."

They'd been sitting across from each other in the fat man's limo near the entrance of Four Seasons Los Angeles, finishing a conversation. This was three weeks ago, maybe a month. The tinted windows and the gray leather seats gave Mrs. Grendel an uneasy feeling. She liked seeing her environment, and she didn't like feeling too comfortable.

"I've heard you're discrete," the fat man said. "A professional."

"I can produce references, if you wish."

"I'm sure." He dismissed the notion with a two-finger wave. "You wouldn't be here if I had misgivings. I don't like misgivings. Who does, am I right?" He didn't wait for her answer. "I like to *know*. It's better for everyone."

"The age of transparency."

"My employers values your discretion," the man said. He was heavyset and a bit jowled, but well-tailored – a light gray striped suit, a beige shirt, a dark tie with white pinpoint spots, very dapper.

"– Employ*ers*?" Mrs. Grendel knew their names, these employ*ers*. If the fat man thought she was a professional, why did he treat her like some stupid shit off the street, an amateur who didn't take time to know her situation? *That's what he thinks of me? Incredible. A man who can't look down and see his own cock.*

"Is the money not sufficient?"

"No, the money's fine. More than fine."

Liesbet Grendel did not go into a project blind. Some did; some preferred not to know. Some would say it was better to keep a target a target, keep it down range and impersonal. Who would want to do it differently? Were you that lonely, did you want a date, a heart-to-heart? Did you really need to discuss the existential implications of what you did before you did it? What would Sartre think, Heidegger, Kierkegaard? Did you want to have that discussion with the person you were going to do it *to*? Mrs. Grendel knew people who had chosen her vocation. Over the years you simply met people; and the consensus was this, *decorate a target with flesh and history and you've complicated your life.*

The gentlemen – and it was *men*; three men, to be exact – who were employing

Mrs. Grendel hadn't been a secret to her. She'd done her homework on the men and the target. The target was a Ms. Silva, Annie Silva, a chubby thing who grew up with daddy in one of those Laurel Canyon red brick and white column homes that belonged more to Colonial Williamsburg than Los Angeles. She was an adult now and had her own home in Brentwood. Lived with a childhood friend until the friend died. The three employers had known the friend, too. Both flesh and history were very important to Liesbet Grendel. No one should go blindly into a kill.

She had picked Annie. She'd known about the gentlemen before they approached her. Who cared about the girl, really. What Liesbet cared about was the girl's work at the Prado.

At the end of her talk with the fat man, before stepping from the limo and going into the Windows Lounge at the Four Seasons, Mrs. Grendel reached over and shook the man's hand. His skin was soft and pink and remarkably cool.

"Give the would be senator my best," she'd said. "– Him and his two idiot friends. Fraternity brothers all, if I remember right."

THEY WERE STILL sitting at a café table beneath the oaks in the Plaza de Santa Ana. Annie hadn't discussed herself that first day with Fr. Rafa at Prado's conservation studio. She didn't plan discussing herself this evening, either. What good would it do? Someone like him, a man who kept the company of his own inventions. "Who needs you cluttering my studio," Annie wanted to say but didn't have the nerve.

"Such a sweet face to look so ..." Fr. Rafa hesitated. Then he said, "I'm not sure what sort of look. Scared?" He tilted his head, considering her. "Maybe not 'scared,' exactly. That's too dramatic for you."

"Excuse me?" *Oh God, a therapist.* "I have my dramatic moments."

He raised a forefinger. "– Anxious. Yes, 'anxious' is the word." As the friar talked his eyebrows had become arched, fretful. He was contemplating her out loud, as if she wasn't privy to his words. *Like I'm a doll with plastic ears,* Annie thought. Then the friar said, "You get my nurturing juices frothy."

"TMI, father," She took another sip of the red.

"What can I say? The curse of a shepherd."

Fr. Rafa was young, Annie figured mid-twenties, ten or eleven years *younger* than her, a boy eager to become an old priest. His black hair had even begun to recede, his forehead pronounced, shiny. Everything about him was locked into an early fragility, the thin fingers and legs, the way his shoulders fold inward to concave his chest.

"I'm all right," she told him and finished off the glass of wine.

"No, no you're not. I don't think so."

From the beginning, the friar had treated her like his flock's troubled lamb. Or maybe he treated everyone like that. She didn't know him well enough to say, though his first impressions were far more negative than positive. Annie particularly disliked being instructed on her own profession. He was who of those men who gave advice whether he knew a fact or not. She'd excellent credentials, a MFA in studio art from the University of Connecticut and another in art conservation from UCLA/Getty. A conservator was a researcher, an academician. Why wouldn't she know her job? Did Fr. Rafa really think she had skipped over 16th Century Flemish Art? A person with Annie's training could go into the Louvre and repair the poplar wood panel of the Mona Lisa, or rid the Grendel painting of its spotty mildew and bring back the original tint and shade, the painting's subtleties. Most conservation programs taught art history, archeology, chemistry – both preventive and treatment techniques – artifact technology, the list was impressive. What Annie liked best was painting. She would rather paint than do most anything, but she had no interest in sharing what she liked with Fr. Rafa.

"I have it under control." That was all Annie had said that first or second morning at Prado's conservation studio.

"Still, my knowledge might be helpful," the friar said. "We should have a drink after work. What do you say? You can ask me questions, pick my brain."

The man wouldn't go away.

Luc Grendel the Elder had completed *Meeting on the Steps to Hades* at the end of the 16th century. This was the painting Annie had reconstructed at her Bentwood home. In those days the pigment was stuck to the linen by glue extracted from animal tissue, not the most pleasant smell.

Did Fr. Rafa know that? She bet not.

"He attempted suicide, you know. Thank God he didn't succeed." The young friar shook his head as he spoke. "A disappointing love, no doubt. Isn't that the usual way with artists?" This had been followed by an audible sigh. He'd been looking over Annie's shoulder that morning at Prado. She stopped her work and glanced up at him, only a moment. He seemed caught in the painting; even did a little shiver. "One can only imagine his suffering."

"I wasn't aware he was so troubled."

"Razor cuts down his forearms."

"– My God." And to herself, "...poor man."

"My point, exactly. But the Lord guided him away from that horrific fate. He lived a long life. I'd have hated to see his immortal soul condemned to the pit."

Annie did not like thinking of herself as a person so quick to judge, particularly a friar, a man of faith, but she'd never met anyone who had such an easy way of combining triumph, voyeurism and pretention in the same breath.

"Who was the woman?" She wanted to know.

"His young bride. Of course the man was definitely a bipolar – obviously more on the depressed side."

"And you know this *how*?"

"Diaries, my dear," Friar Rafa said. Annie could've also done without the "my dear" thing from a twenty-something. She imagined him as a boy dressed up in his father's clothes. "This painter *loved* diaries," he said. "Diaries written in English, I might add. Along with being a bipolar, he was a very secretive man. Few Dutch spoke English then, you know. French, yes. English, not so much. So maybe paranoid, too.

Who knows, I'm not a psychologist."

"I'm glad you get that."

"Pardon? 'Get' what?"

"– Your limits."

The painting certainly would disturb any passerby who stopped to consider its creatures, its dark territory. The friar wasn't alone. Annie had felt the pull, too; dreamt about the picture once or twice. Demons of all types gathered on those spiraled gray steps. Some showed their claws and yellow teeth. Some had pinned their victims to the stairs and walls and opened them from throat to crotch, entrails collapsing across the gray stone. Each demon appeared different than the next – winged creatures, ones with scales and red eyes, ones who looked almost human except for their wide mouths and black tongues, so on and so on. Tiny slits, circles and half moons had been cut into the gold doors that lined the downward turn and shadow of the stairway. Blood speckled both gold and stone. Creatures were also in the rooms behind the doors. Annie could see their silver eyes through the openings.

"I'd like to look at the diaries," Annie had said.

"Ah, see. I'll be helping you after all."

SHE COULD TELL the boy was getting tired now – her apprentice Bullfighter, her *torero* from the Escuela Taurina de Madrid. Mrs. Grendel had watched the boy for almost two hours. He'd been practicing turns with his scarlet cape beneath the lamplight in the Casa de Campo. Occasionally one of the prostitutes would stop and attempt to chat with him but he ignored them. Mrs. Grendel thought the boy seemed shy. He was at that age where perhaps he believed desire could reveal his foolishness. Later he'd go home and stroke himself and think how talking with a prostitute had many endings and how a nod or smile might have changed his life.

Gone was the humidity of the evening. This night had a chill to it. Liesbet still sat on the wood next to a cluster of pines, her white cape tucked about her shoulders and arms. She'd been thinking about the would-be senator who'd hired her, Taylor Bane, and the two men who were the closest to him, an Eddy somebody and a third asshole by the name of Bailey

Sutton. The fat man didn't need to reveal the names of her employers. Did he think she wouldn't know, that she'd walk into a situation – *any* situation – unprepared? He was as foolish as the little *torero* under the lamplight.

When these employers were boys they belonged to the same fraternity at a small rich kid's college in the Santa Barbara area of California. This was the fraternity that put together the 1991 Halloween party where two high school girls were beaten and raped, a fourteen-year-old and a fifteen-year-old. Everybody was drunk and the boys had worn masks, gray alien masks with big dark eyes. Taylor and his friends were never caught, of course, rich boys and richer fathers. The fourteen-year-old girl died last year of breast cancer at the age of thirty-four. Both girls had been chained to metal cots and vaginally and anally penetrated many times. Cocks and broom handles were used, as Mrs. Grendel understood it. The fifteen-year-old suffered after effects that included auditory and visual hallucinations – preferring to believe an alien abduction complete with anal probe, rather than the evil that had truly happened – and she'd been hospitalized for three years.

That girl was Annie Silva.

"– Time to train," Mrs. Grendel whispered to herself.

She stood, a chilled breeze flapping the edges of her cape. The night was starry and the area about the yellow lamplight had no traffic. The boy stepped away from the light to rest, his back facing her.

A very tired boy, Mrs. Grendel thought and secured the cape about her arms as she walked down the path toward him. *A boy who worked too hard, too long. And for what? For nothing.*

She passed close to him and saw the perspiration on his neck and the collar of his white shirt. A beat or two after passing the boy, the woman heard him fall but she didn't stop walking.

Liesbet Grendel liked to compare herself to a cellist who didn't need to look at her hands or her bow to do the job. Practice is the key – in and out, in and out. She'd grasped the pearl handle of the pick and pressed it through the boy's back, between the sixth and seventh ribs and into the edge of his left lung and the left atrium of his heart. She had done this before.

2

Calle de Antoni Maura
Madrid, Spain

An evening with the conservator

"DID YOU FORGIVE me and I just didn't notice?"

Annie was looking at the painting she'd done of Mariel, talking to it, wanting to hear her own thoughts out loud. What she truly wanted was to have the painting talk back to her; to hear *Mariel* again, a sentence, a word. Annie had the portrait shipped from their Brentwood home to her apartment in Madrid and it had arrived yesterday. She'd finished the piece in early June – three months ago – and Mariel had died the last week of July.

"I couldn't ask you the question," Annie whispered. Eleven-thirty in the morning on a Saturday and she was sipping her second glass of red. *Ahh, real good; real sane. Lose weight, pass out before lunch.* "Why couldn't I say, 'Do you forgive me?' How very chicken shit not to do that, or very *some*thing. But close as we were, Mariel, I didn't have the courage."

Too much to lose, that's what your mom said.

The apartment on the Calle de Antoni Maura was less than two blocks from the Prado, a ten-minute walk if Annie did it right. The apartment had a skylight, three floor-to-ceiling windows and a cedar floor. It was a long narrow room with a kitchenette to the left and a bed and bath area opposite the entrance way. Annie knew painters who would kill for less. No sunlight and no cloud left the room untouched. On the white walls in the living area were five large photos of the Grendel painting, *Meeting on the Steps to Hades*, sections where damage had occurred – spots of dirty faded color, the worn linen, the effects of the paint on the linen, the effect of the weather on it all, much to repair.

Annie was now sitting cross-legged at the foot of the bed, sipping her red. The wine went down smooth and warm. *This stuff is far too good.* She remembered how her mother and dad used to argue about her mother's drinking. Constantly. *See, I blame you, Mommy. It's my 'What-Can-I-Do?-It's-Genetic.' excuse.*

The acrylic painting of Mariel hung on the wall opposite her. Annie had placed it there yesterday. Mariel was nothing but bleached bone – that's how she was then, bone and shiny skin – the remainder of her dark hair shaved close to the skull. In the painting she lay on rumpled ivory sheets and looked out a half-opened window.

"I can imagine you giving me one of your Get Real smiles," Annie said, the hem of her cotton bath robe draped her thick pale calf. *A little too thick, if you ask me. There are no wine diets for a reason.* Late morning light came through the windows in wide yellow columns that showed bits of dust. She'd a hand over her brow to block the sun. "I was the sensitive one," Annie said, eyes squinted, looking at her painting. "That's what you called me. And you were always the what – the cynical one? Remember how we did that with the Beatles – Paul was the cute one, and Ringo was the funny one? I mean who cared if they were popular years ago, we loved them anyway."

Annie's short blond hair was pulled back and tied off with a red rubber band. She would have *loved* a cigarette, even after eleven months of abstaining. Mariel had smoked and second-hand smoke wasn't much different than second hand suffering, both were infectious.

"I ought to spend my time in healthier ways," Annie scolded herself. *Not only the wine, my stupid thoughts, too.* She couldn't stop obsessing about the fraternity party, all those years ago now – Halloween, 1991 – and the many chances she'd had to apologize for dragging Mariel along with her.

What's wrong with older guys? She had said, age fifteen. *Let's have some fun. High school boys are so, I dunno, tedious. Seriously, Mariel, how long have we been talking about that – Johnny Waterfield and that other jerk wad? What's-his name, the one with the Mohawk? Whoever heard of a Jew with a Mohawk. These guys are like studies in immaturity or something.*

Mariel had died on a sunny cloudless day. After the cancer had taken both her breasts it had taken her life and it had left Annie dark in grief. *What are you doing to yourself?* She looked down at her glass of red, a sip or two shy of empty. "Bring out the whips and chains and be done with it," Annie said and finished the wine.

Enough, enough.

A small package was on the mahogany nightstand. A messenger from Prado had brought over the Luc Grendel's diary and she had not bothered to open it. Fr. Rafa had promised Annie he would do that and, no matter what she thought of the man, Fr. Rafa did what he promised. The Grendel diary came wrapped in brown paper and tied with twine and could have been a box of anything. The messenger who delivered the diary spoke little to no English and tried to come on to her, weave his magic. He couldn't have been more than nineteen or twenty, a cute boy with a wisp or two of dark hair on his chin and upper lip.

"*Hoy no, poco Remo*," she'd said.

"– When then, Miss?"

"YOU WALK THIS earth like you're a visitor in somebody else's home," her father had said. This was right after the Halloween party, Annie a month or so into her fifteenth year. Her father the great Ben Silva – "Big Ben," a man adored, ask the folks who knew him. And, yes, he was like the clock, big and loud and on time. Growing up, Annie saw him as a flamboyant bear with untamable dark hair and wire rim glasses, a slap-your-back sort who loved wearing Hawaiian shirts, baggy khakis and two-tone shoes.

"What does your father do, Annie?"

Mrs. Halfner was asking the class about what their mothers and fathers did for a living. Ethel Halfner had delicate features with pointy cheek bones and chin, black framed glasses and hose that always looked wrinkled. She'd been Annie's fifth grade teacher who, on that day, was searching for another Show and Tell Parent.

"He draws backgrounds," Annie told her.

"What on earth?" Her teacher's face seemed to unravel.

"– For Mr. Disney."

Then an ah-ha grin appeared. "Oh. *Really*?"

Big Ben Silva had come to his child's school and wowed the Show and Tell crowd.

Their first father-daughter talk began two days after Annie had been admitted to

Holstein-Cromwell. This was a children's hospital for "helping your child learn crisis management" as the brochure said, a modern glass and steel building fifteen miles north of Monterey.

Annie didn't want to hear Big Ben. She was still fighting off the Grays, aliens with broad skulls and gigantic black almond-shaped eyes. She was sure they'd enjoyed probing her far too much to give up so quickly. On that second day Annie was in four-point restraint, her hands and feet strapped to the bed. She believed the staff was preparing her for another examination by the Grays.

"Get me out of here," Annie said to Ben, panicked, a raw whisper. She was out of breath from the crying and the fear. Her face and body were bruised, her left eye swollen shut. "Untie me, Daddy. *Please*, please. I'll be good, I promise."

"You *are* good, sweetheart." Ben sat on the edge of her bed. He wanted to be strong for his daughter but he could feel his tears getting ready to show themselves. When he tried to stroke her hair, Annie jerked her head away, as if she was afraid he'd strike her. "Okay, okay, Pal." He put his two hands in the air, hold-up style. "No touching, I get it. Sorry. What can I say, I'm a big dope when it comes to this sort of stuff."

"They were *real*, Daddy." Her shoulders had a tremble.

"Take a breath. See if you can get calm."

"I *saw* their faces." Annie was looking out the window, to the right of her bed. A breeze came into the room, billowing the peach colored curtains.

Early morning...maybe Late October, that she knew.

The psychiatric aide would ask her the same questions each morning. *What is the date, Annie? Do you know the year?* His name was Michael and he had beautiful tanned skin and sort of Asian eyes with long lashes. He had a soft voice, too. *Can you tell me the month? What about your address, where do you live?*

"– Maybe hell," she said to the last question, partly joking, partly not. "Where do you live, Michael?

He laughed, the same softness as his talk.

"Some days the same."

"So we're neighbors."

"Fo'sure, girl."

That morning Ben and Annie were alone. If she wanted to talk, he would let her talk. "Just listen," Annie's doc had told him. "People like to be heard. They may plead with you to solve every problem on planet Earth but you don't need to go there. People simply want to be understood."

Ben *did* want to solve Annie's problems, make them go away, have her happy and without a bruise. *That's what we do, isn't it? Fathers – give us a situation and we'll tell you how to solve it. We'll rewind the clock and bring back a bruiseless child.* He found sitting and listening more difficult than he'd imagined. Hard to believe that what felt like nothing could really be something.

"I think I saw them at the Halloween party." Annie was still looking at the peach colored curtains move to an on-again off-again breeze. "The 'Grays.' Isn't that what they're called? They bury their spaceships under the ground or hide them deep in the woods, I read about it. Those ships are *so* cold, daddy. So damp and dark." He didn't think his daughter had got this from reading about it. She had *felt* it. She had *seen* it. She'd laid on their tables and dealt with their operating equipment. Or *thought* she had, Ben understood that truth by her small trembling body, by the urgency of her voice. Annie turned to look at him. "I'm sure the Grays were at the party. Everybody had on a costume. But I think they came as themselves."

ANNIE HADN'T WANTED to leave Mariel's picture alone in their house. Or maybe – and this was closer to the truth – Annie hadn't wanted to be in Spain without Mariel.

"You're the sentimental one," Mariel had liked to say. The Beatle Game, match a person you know to a Beatle personality. Annie and Mariel made up the game when they were classmates in Monterey Elementary.

Which Beatle does that make me? Was there ever a sentimental Beatle?

Paul – it had to be. Paul wasn't merely the cute one; wasn't just another pretty face. No, he wrote "Yesterday" and "Michelle"– mostly written by him – and "Silly Love Songs." Yeah, Paul was cute AND also totally sentimental.

"Sont des mots qui vont tres bien ensemble!"

Ha!

"I must be Paul," Annie had said to her, this years later at their Brentwood house.

"You – you are John, Mariel. Cynical, clever, John, that's *so* you. All rebellious, a social conscience. You'd write "Give Peace a Chance" and "Imagine." You'd get tangled up with an Artsy type like me."

I am Paul and I am Yoko.

goo goo g'joob

There had never been a Ringo, though. Or a George, the spiritual one. *Isn't that Odd? My apologies, Ringo and George. My deep, heart-felt apologies. I think Mariel and I loved you two most of all. You were both so rare – like the first warm day after winter. What can I say? It's hard to find a trustworthy confessor or good clown when you need one.*

They had talked about going to Madrid together less than a month before Mariel died. The best Annie could do was have the portrait of Mariel shipped to the Madrid apartment.

Sunlight still flooded the long and narrow room from everywhere – the skylight and the floor to ceiling windows, very bright, very yellow and dusty – light stopped by the flat of Annie's palm. Below her apartment was the Calle de Antoni Maura with its shady trees and early afternoon traffic. She hadn't moved from the foot of the bed, her focus on the painting of Mariel above the headboard. Nothing ever got between her and Mariel, not even the sunlight.

"That night, I heard you screaming." Annie's voice was barely audible. She held a half glass of the red in her left hand, the bottle on the nightstand next to the small package wrapped in brown paper, what the messenger had delivered that morning. "You seemed far away – another country, another planet. I could hear how they were hurting you, and I knew they must be hurting you the way they were hurting me. I remember thinking, 'they must've tied her down and torn off her pretty costume.' Didn't we have such pretty costumes that night?"

–The sentimental one.

"They were lovely, our costumes." Annie stopped. Abruptly her vision blurred.

She felt tears hot on her face. "Could you hear me, too?"

DR. DANIEL PENSKE was Annie's doc at Holstein-Cromwell and the one who had told her father to "–Just listen to your daughter, okay?" Dan Penske had the look of a forty-year-old who might have been a pretty good athlete in his college days; wrestling, maybe; something for stocky and low to the ground types. He wore tortoise-shell glasses and had a dark stubble-close haircut.

"I need to talk with you about your daughter," Dr. Penske said. He and Ben were outside the closed door of the girl's hospital room. A florescent light had started to hum and flicker. It gave a shaky feeling to the marble hallway. "How Annie's is explaining her experience isn't out of the ordinary."

"I don't believe in alien shit," Ben said.

"There's a link – statistically I mean – between childhood abuse and people who think they've been abducted," Dr. Penske said. He'd been reviewing Annie's chart and he stopped to look at Ben. "Most abuse is done by family, relatives, that sort of thing. I don't know, maybe it's safer to think aliens are the villains than the people who should be caring and protecting you. These abduction stories have amazing similarities – paralysis, flashing lights, buzzing sounds, electrical sensations. There's most always lots of probing, too. The whole touching, poking stuff is all part of it."

"– And rape," Ben said.

"...yeah. That."

"Child Protective Services came to the house," Ben said. "Some lady, a social worker, I think, who knows. Wanted to check and see if I provided a safe environment.

Me, the *father*. Is that unbelievable, or what? We got a very nice home, Doc. I mean I do okay."

"They're a tough group, naturally suspicious."

"– Annie and her friend go to this fraternity party." Ben didn't want to get *more* paranoid about his CPS interrogation. He could feel himself getting annoyed at the well-meaning Penske for simply being willing to discuss them. "You think Annie tells me everything? What kid does that? How 'bout *your* kids

– they do that?" He didn't wait for an answer. "A parent can't keep track."

"I got two teenage boys, Ben. I get it."

"– Blaming *me*, this social worker, whoever." His voice was quiet but intense. "Why am I being blamed? Am I supposed to follow my daughter everywhere? Be a mind reader?"

"Did they really blame you?"

"Well maybe 'blame' is too strong. But it damn well *felt* that way."

On the day Ben left his job at Disney, he'd come home all excited, wanting to tell Annie how he and four other animators were going to start their own company, do stories that interested them. He wanted to share his happiness with her. Ben only managed a few sentences before his girl and her friend, Mariel, trotted off to Pointer's College and that fraternity party – not that he had known where they were going at the time, not that he hadn't *tried* to find out.

"We talk ourselves out of living," he'd said to his daughter and Mariel, excited about his day, his future. "People will invent you, Annie, if you don't show up. If you don't say, 'This is me. This is *who* I am. This is *what* I do.' You think other people will give a shit, if you don't? No they will not, no, ma'am, no how, no way."

"That's great, daddy." Annie was less than interested.

"So what's with the get-ups?" he'd wanted to know.

Both Annie and Mariel had worn blue and turquoise kimonos that night, kimonos bought at the Green Earth Consignment on Prescott near the Presidio. They'd powdered their faces white and they had fixed their hair alike, too – pushed up and pinned, a wooden chopstick stuck through a bun.

"– Geishas," Annie said.

"It's like a Halloween party," Mariel said.

By that time they were at the front door.

"Hey, Annie, give me a time frame. *Some*thing." Ben heard the concern in his voice; a bit whiny, too.

"Daddy, I'm not a child."

"I need a phone number, something."

"I'll *call* you, okay?" She rolled her eyes, so easily exasperated.

"And give me a number."

"Yeah, okay. A number."

Ben thought it was a party in the neighborhood. Kids in her class, that sort of thing, a *chaperoned* party with a mother or a father, preferably both. Responsible *older* people who would herd in the hormones, that was what he had in mind.

Fourteen and fifteen going to a fraternity party. What could possibly go wrong? Drinking, doing God-knows-what. Don't kids put two and two together? What did they think would happen?

Big Ben Silva liked to say the beginning of his father-daughter talks really had to do with leaving Disney and racing off the cliff to spark his fate and fortune, him and the four other animators – the Jolly Gents, what they liked to call themselves. After that day everybody became Five Bohemian Productions and the once Jolly Gents began cranking out the sort of animation that told you secrets about yourself. And always funny, always insightful, always human. They were *that* good, better than Big Ben Silva expected, and *nobody* –no-bod-*eee*–was laughing.

This is who I am. This is what I do.

"– Not what a parent wants to hear," Dr. Penske was saying, meaning the CPS's suspiciousness during their recent interview with Ben.

"I'm *no* criminal," The big man told him, serious to the point of grave. Then he grinned. "God, I sound like Nixon."

ANNIE DIDN'T BELIEVE their father-daughter talks had started with Big Ben leaving his bi-monthly paycheck to start a business. Five Bohemian Productions was real enough, the money, the accolades, those wonderfully sweet and funny stories that showed confused people ultimately helping each other, all of it very real – especially the *money*. They bought a bigger house in Laurel Canyon near Mulholland, a much bigger house, the sort of brick and white column home seen in Virginia – Charlottesville, Williamsburg, a colonial of sorts – but sprawled out and surrounded by palms and Yucca plants. Only a bipolar could spend Hollywood money at the speed it needed to be spent, and Ben Silva tried his best. In those days Big Ben had told himself many lies and bought himself and his daughter many things. That time had been very rough for both Annie and Ben. Annie didn't think about motives at fifteen but later she had thought a lot about motives. Their father-daughter talks began after Annie's mom, Jean Lynn Silva, left them to marry Buster Connors, the man she'd been sneaking a fuck with for close to two years.

Annie was still in her Madrid apartment, sitting cross-legged on the bed. Her thoughts had briefly gone to Big Ben and her nightmare Halloween party. But now she stared at the painting of a naked Mariel laying on a wrinkled sheet and looking out an opened window. It abruptly brought Annie to tears. After almost two hours and a nearly finished bottle of red, her tears showed like a late but frantic dinner guest.

Her pretty bones, Annie thought, the back of her hand wiping her face. She still sat at the foot of the bed. *All that white skin and blue veins just hugging her bones – her rib cage, the slender fingers, her long sharp legs – such a beautiful skeleton.*

Pouring what remained of the red into her glass – the last swallow, a quarter inch maybe less – Annie drank it right away. She reached for the Luc Grendel diary on her nightstand, pulling at the twine, unwrapping the brown paper. The diary's cover was a rough tan leather, the size of a paperback, the name LUC burned into it. The book had been made by hand, the pages a stiff yellowed linen, probably what the man had used for his paintings. There were pencil sketches on the first and second pages, small drawings but very detailed, heads with grinning faces and dark crooked teeth. The ears reminded Annie of Mr. Spock on *Star Trek*. Their ears were pointed and had veins that puffed the surface of the skin. Above their foreheads and lush curls were small but visible bumps, similar to the horns of a young lamb.

The first line of the diary brought a chill across Annie's shoulders.

Roeselare, West Flanders

Zomer, 1567

I am Luc Grendel, and I know where the demons live.

3

Dr. Zeke Frieder's Office
Carmel, California

Taylor Bane's wife goes to therapy

"TAYLOR? GO TO therapy? Oh, *ple*ase." Winifred Bane did what she called a "pig snort." Immediately her fingertips pressed her lips as if to stop the possibility of another one. The woman was an inch shy of six feet and wore a pale gray suit and a silk coffee colored blouse. Her red hair was combed back and into a twist. "Maybe if you had your therapy on a golf course," Mrs. Bane said. "– The nineteenth hole, next to the bar. Then maybe he'd grace you with his divine presence, but I certainly wouldn't count on it, darling."

"You have a nice sense of humor," Dr. Ezekiel Frieder said – his first impression of her – and he smiled, showing pink gums.

"I must. At one time I wanted to have his child." Mrs. Bane also had on large round sunglasses that hid most of her face. "But that was more than a few years ago."

"I'm just saying marital therapy is best done with the couple." Dr. Frieder wasn't sure when he was going to mention her sunglasses but he was definitely going to mention them. "How do you like being addressed? Last name, first name, what shall it be?"

"Fred – Like in Wini*fred*. Or Freddie, I like that, too." Fred crossed her legs at the knee and absently wiggled her foot and looked away from him. The window was open and there was the sound of afternoon traffic and, in the distance, she could see the blue-green water of Carmel Bay. "Since Taylor refused to have therapy with me, I decided to go myself."

"Good for you."

Dr. Frieder then told his patient to say whatever came to her mind and when he had something to contribute he would let her know.

The psychologist looked early fifties, maybe fifty-five. He had the scuffed brown loafer and tweedy appearance of an academic. His hair was full but cobbled together like unruly twigs, a mix of gray and brown. There was also the matter with his hands. He'd always thought his hands were too small and delicate for a man.

"– Is it?" Fred said, considering her new therapist.

"Is it what?"

"Good for me?"

"Well someone hit you, didn't they?"

"I'M RUNNING FOR the senate in November," Taylor Bane had said when Fred suggested couples therapy. He was a tall, six-four or five, and had a crafted stylishness about himself. He sat in their living room on a leather high-back chair, his right elbow on the armrest, the white cuff of his shirt precisely a quarter inch above the sleeve of a navy-blue suit jacket. His legs were crossed. The trousers had a perfect crease and the crossed pant leg was draped ever so slightly over polished black wingtips. "You *know* I'm in this race, that I have bigger plans for us than the senate. What's between your ears – cotton, mush? – what the fuck is it? I know it's nothing to do with a brain. What do you think would happen if the voters discovered I'd been in therapy? *Therapy*, for Christ-sake."

"I don't know, Taylor. Think you were an actual person?"

"Excuse me?"

"– An *act*ual person." Like are you deaf?

Sunshine came through the open living room windows, white and brilliant on the pine polyurethane floor, the beige lacquered walls. Seagulls were nestled at the edge of the lawn where the grass stopped and a cloudless sky began. Beyond the drop-off was the blue water and the occasional sailboat of the bay.

"What the fuck world do you live in, Freddie?" His tone was calm, even. The word "kindly" came to her mind. *Yes, that's it. Kindly.* And always the handsome boy, brown hair slicked back without a part, lazy brown eyes. Her husband said, "Voters think I'm an 'actual' person if I bowl or cut my own grass. If I'm in therapy, they'll think I'm a crazy asshole who can't handle his own marriage, so how in the hell can I handle their concerns – that's what they'd think. Do you *get* that, do you understand? You are just an incredibly naïve fuck, Freddie."

"Don't curse at me."

"Or you'll what?"

"You know I don't like it when you curse at me."

"Or you'll do *what*?"

"Just don't do it, please."

Taylor Bane stood and adjusted a shirt cuff and the sleeve of his suit. He walked over to the green and silver brocaded Victorian sofa – that should have been at least ten thousand less than what he'd paid – and he slapped his wife's face with the flat of his hand and all his considerable strength.

"You want to be a senator's lady?" he whispered.

Freddie's head was bowed as if she was taking a good look at a floor she'd seen a million times. Both hands hovered above her head.

"– Please."

"Shut the fuck up."

She kept quiet.

"Now I'm asking a question here." Taylor Bane collected his emotions while fingering the double Windsor of his red and blue striped tie. "Most women would sell their souls to be with the lawmakers of this great country, our dear and glorious America. How 'bout you, Fred? Sweet, sweet, Freddie. Where are *you* on this issue? The American people want to know. Would you like to be the senator's lady?"

"– Yes, I'd like that."

"See? This is all we want to know. It's that fucking simple."

"DO YOU ALWAYS wear your sunglass indoors?" Dr. Frieder tried to sound casual, a chit-chat among friends.

There was sunlight in his office, yes, but also islands of shadow. Winifred Bane and Ezekiel Frieder sat in identical tan velour chairs across from one another, a narrow teak wood coffee table between them. Fred was in the shadier part of the room. *Now or never, isn't it?* Zeke thought. *No deceptions, please. Let us take the glasses off and talk about the bruises.*

I'd like to pick another topic," she said.

"Abused Wives for six hundred?"

"... w-what?"

"Freddie, this isn't a quiz show."

"We could talk about my college days." The big sunglasses showed only her chin and cheekbones and her lipstick red lips. Anxiety quivered the edges of her words. "I met Taylor at Pointer, you know. We were college sweethearts. Don't you think that's romantic?"

"Tell me about the glasses."

"– God you're like a pit bull." Being playful but meaning it. A fleck of lipstick spotted her left front tooth, that lovely smile. "It's my sensitive eyes, nothing complex. I'm *not* a complicated person, believe me. I should have been born in the south, that's what Taylor says. 'Such a delicate flower,' he says. I'm told I bruise like that girl in the *Princess and the Pea.*"

"Who said that?"

"It's a favorite of Taylor's – you know, where a pea is under the mattress and in the morning the princess is covered with bruises. You know the one. It's such a silly little story."

"I do know it. How long has he been beating you?"

Winifred Bane kept quiet but with the same lovely smile.

"Taylor. How long has he been slapping you around?" Dr. Frieder's voice was gentle, close to a whisper. People hated looking at many things about themselves and being abused was the sort of secret even the abused didn't want to know.

Mrs. Bane's expression went from her red lipstick smile to horrified. "Oh you've got it *wrong*. Taylor's a kind, generous man."

"– How long?"

"I won't stay and listen to this. I'm sorry." She stood, brushing something invisible from the right thigh of her pale gray pant leg.

"This is your chance, Fred." Dr. Frieder leaned in, the sides of his arms resting just above his knees as he watched her. "Be courageous. Let someone else in on your secret. I know it isn't easy. But people do it all the time, and a few have done it from that very chair."

"– You're mistaken. I know you mean well."

"I make a lot of mistakes, you're right." Zeke leaned back and propped his folded hands on his slight belly. "You're absolutely right. My wife – who I adore more than my own life – tells me this at least once a week. But what I'm saying to you now isn't one of them, isn't a mistake, is it? What do you think, Freddie? Do you think my wife would add this to her list, or would she let me have this one? Would she say, 'When you're right you're right.' What do you think?"

"WHAT'S THE WOMAN'S name?" Taylor Bane wanted to know. There were two other men with him in his second-floor study, confidants since their college days.

"Liesbet Grendel. Very professional," one of the men said. He was the fat one with the tight gabardine. His suit vest struggled to contain him. The man had a balding spot surrounded by short dark curls. "Oh you know Liesbet," he said. "Sweet disposition, respectful. Uses a pick."

"We hired her before," the third one added. The third one looked reasonable, nice pinstripe, trimmed mustache. He was in his late thirties, near the ages of Taylor and the fat man.

Fred had not meant to listen but she was passing the study and the door was open. Unlike the rest of the house – big windows and lots of sunshine – Taylor's study had a cave-ish gloom to it. A glance into her husband's Neanderthalic side. Everything was dark cherry wood and Persian carpeting. Two glass doors to a small open terrace were draped with slate-colored velvet curtains. Winifred always imagined campfires in this room, red-orange sparks drifting upward and breaking apart the shadows. Caveman shit, Taylor's *forte,* not even brandy and cigars, not for

Taylor. Her hubby was raw meat and blood on the chin. Guttural noise and the tossing of fresh bones. Sexy in its way, if a girl was honest. Freddie was not an eavesdropper but what was a wife supposed to do – *not* walk through her own home, go here but never go there? She couldn't be expected to remember every rule, the dos, the don'ts. His wife lived here too, didn't she?

So Mrs. Bane *heard* things. On occasion.

Pointer College buddies, that's how he'd first introduced the two men, years ago now – same liberal arts classes, finger-painting their way through Western Civ, the same fraternity, all for one and one for all, Kappa Kappa Obnoxious. Bailey Sutton was just as fat in his younger days – but pinker, much pinker, so very cheery in his pinkness. He had puffy pink hands and slick puffy pink cheeks.

"How does he have sex?" She'd been curious.

"I didn't know you liked fat boys."

"It's a logistics question, Taylor."

"I'm guessing with his dick."

The third one, the regular looking guy, he was Eddy Whoever. *Shit. C'mon.*

Phillips. Yes, tedious Eddy Phillips. People actually called him Boring Eddy. He wasn't the sort anyone remembered, too average-looking, too quiet, too beige.

So perfect for his job.

"– Kill her," Boring Eddy was saying. "You kill her, you get the bitch out of the way. Very simple, really. Then it's a clean drive home. Am I right?"

WINIFRED BANE HAD removed the sunglasses but she was looking at her lap, the pale gray pants, and avoiding Dr. Frieder who sat across from her.

"– Satisfied?" she said, pouty, barely audible.

"You have a lovely face."

"It's been lovelier."

When Freddie did raise her head, she looked out the office window and not at the doctor. Three very white gulls glided above Carmel Bay. Thick dark clouds were coming in from the northwest.

"What does he hit you with?"

She couldn't believe how beautiful the gulls were against the clouded sky.

"– Freddie?"

"His fists."

"Nothing else?

"His fists are plenty," she said, turning to him. There was a green-purple mark that went from above the outside edge of her right eyebrow and around the outside corner of her eye and ended at the mid-point below the bottom lash. "He says he boxed in college. I don't remember him doing that. Boxing. But that's what he tells me. He tells his friends that, too. Maybe it's true. Or Maybe he's just said it enough to believe it."

"Have you thought of leaving?"

"He doesn't like to lose."

"What does that mean?" Dr. Frieder knew what it meant.

Fred was looking out the window again. The gulls had disappeared and the clouds were dark. Then she said, "My husband likes talking about himself in third person. 'Nobody fucks with Taylor Bane' is one of his favorites."

"You can't have a conversation?"

"That would be way too normal."

There were small wood tables next to their leather chairs. Fred's table had a box of tissues and a silver tray with a pitcher of water and an empty glass. Zeke Frieder had several paperbacks on his table and a yellow legal pad for notes. He'd never used the legal pad, preferring to dictate into a recorder after each session. Still, he liked the look of it there. Zeke imagined his patients thinking, *Well the old asshole hasn't used the pad yet, I must be doing okay.*

"What's the worst?" Dr. Frieder said.

"That's he's done? Shit I don't know, I got thrown across the room once." She pointed to the outside corner of her bruised eye. "You can't see it right now but I hit the piano bench and had to get a couple of stitches."

"Taylor is a dangerous fellow."

"He hasn't stabbed me," Freddie said. She tried to laugh but couldn't do it.

"Ah. So a good marriage."

"I'm glad you find my life amusing."

"I don't find your life amusing. I think you're life's a horror story." Dr. Frieder took the yellow pad from the table and began writing. It was "Mary had a Little Lamb," actually. But Fred couldn't see it. Zeke Frieder knew his patient would only see him just getting serious with the pad. "One day he will kill you," Frieder said. "Maybe he won't mean to. Probably he won't. He might even feel terrible about it. You know, cry at the funeral. Show his love and all."

"– God."

"You need to wake up, Freddie."

4

Museo del Prado
Madrid, Spain

Annie's try at babysitting

ANNIE HAD FOUND Beth Lee outside the book and gift shop on the first floor of the museum. The child sat cross-legged near the shop's entrance amid the gray marble and the sunlight from the windows and a vast open space. Her eyes and cheeks were pink from crying. *Who left you alone*? That was Annie's first thought. The child must have been five or six. She had the sickly look of an orphan in some tale by Dickens – *Oliver Twist*, perhaps. Her narrow pretty face was marked with shadow beneath the cheekbones and the eyes. Uneven wisps of blond hair edged a rainbow-colored skullcap. Her denim sundress was two sizes more than she needed, conceivably an older sister's toss-away.

Have I imagined finding another sick one? What do you say, is that you, baby girl? Are you my new Mariel?

"– Mama's lost," Beth Lee had managed to say. Her arms and legs were more bone than flesh.

Annie had scooped up the child; telling her, "Shh, shh, it's okay, it's all right.

We'll find your mommy. It's okay, hon, I promise."

Immediately there were more thoughts of Mariel.

You're the skinny George Beatle, aren't you? Annie kissed the girl's cheek – a dry, surprisingly fragile cheek – and carried her across the marble floor to the information booth. *Not the young, spiritual George, that's not you. No, no. You're the one that came later, the sick, vulnerable one.*

Playing the Beatle game again, the way she and Mariel had done.

"So who am I now?" Mariel liked to say. Naked on crumpled sheets, showing her bones. "Which Beatle? Wait, wait, don't say a word. I must be Sick George. Isn't that right, isn't that what you're thinking?"

BETH LEE TOUCHED the worn leather cover of the Grendel diary with the tip of her index finger. She did this cautiously, as if it was a small but dangerous animal who'd have her fingers for lunch.

"It's a diary," Annie said. The book was on a wood table beside one of the large windows in the conservation studio. There were five large windows and two skylights in the room. The glass and the white walls allowed the studio a brilliant, full light. Annie had decided to bring the child here to wait for the mother. "Be careful, honey, it's a very old. You know what a diary is?"

Beth Lee shook her head, she didn't.

"People write about their lives in dairies," Annie said. She was talking while she worked on the Grendel painting, adding an umber color in the shadow of the stairway. "Their thoughts, too. When I was a girl I had a diary, I wrote down every thought in my head – how important those thoughts seemed. A few still are, but not many." Annie nodded toward the leather book on the table next to Beth Lee. "– That one belonged to

Mr. Grendel, the man who painted this picture."

"Is the diary scary like his picture?"

"– Very scary, yes."

"Will you read some to me?"

Annie was working on correcting the bottom right quarter fades of *Meeting on Steps to Hades,* spotty bleached areas. She ignored the girl's question and waited for her to have other thoughts and other questions. Beth Lee sat on a wood and leather stool not too far away from Annie. The child was surprisingly quiet. The demons in the right quarter had faded ears and hands and feet. Their teeth also needed attention. The teeth blurred into the mouth. Grendel's original painting had needle pointed teeth, very long and sharp, the sort of teeth that can pin you down and take your life. Restoring a painting was never easy, especially this one, but Annie loved working at Prado's. It was most always sunlit and cheerful.

"Why're you doin' that?" Beth Lee said, the quiet snapping in two. Her voice was extra loud, what her mother called "an outside voice," and the child touched a finger to her lips to shush herself. She said with her softest voice, "It's a scary picture."

"Pictures can't hurt us."

"It can scare the children."

A moment or two of quiet went by before Annie said, "– Are you sick, honey?"

The words came out before she could stop them. If the child was sick, maybe reminding her wasn't the best idea. *Who wants to be reminded of terrible things?* Annie hated to upset anyone, especially kids.

For the third time a woman on the PA system was requesting Beth Lee's mom, Mrs. Heather Latterimer, to go to the information desk. The woman on the PA also said they'd found her daughter Beth Lee.

"I'm *not* lost," Beth Lee said. "I'm in Madrid. Mama said since I'm sick we need to look at pretty things and go to interesting places."

"Where are you and your mom from?"

"– Wisconsin!" The girl said it very loudly. "Madison, Wisconsin! Want to hear my address?" Beth didn't wait for an answer. "– One-seven-eight Hurley Avenue. In

Madison!"

"So you're *definitely* not lost."

"... she isn't looking for me." The tone to her words was soft, resigned.

"You mother? Of course she's looking for you."

"No. She never looks for me."

Annie didn't know what to say.

"Mama has bad nerves." The girl folded her skinny arms and gave Annie a firm quick nod as if to say that was the truth and she wasn't budging from it. "Mama says I happen to be a very sick, sick person," Beth Lee said, as if bewildered by it all. "I have the –" she stopped and whispered, "– *cancer*. That's how Mama says it, really quiet. *Cancer*. Like it's asleep."

Is everybody dying from this terrible shit?

Annie stood, pressed her fingers to the small of her back. She walked to the window, looking down at the park across the street, the narrow tan graveled paths, the immaculate lawn. Madrid had a lot of parks, all of them well kept. Sunlight went between the branches of the pink almond trees.

Is that true? Does Heather Latterimer never look for her daughter?

Never?

It didn't seem out of the question, a mother getting up one morning and plotting how she'd run from her dying, cancerous baby. Hadn't Annie thought that more than once with Mariel? Who wanted to see a beloved child or companion die? Let them die in peace, what some on-lookers say. Translation: let them die without me watching them die.

Why exactly are you dying on me, anyway? Isn't that the thought? If we cut into the dark part of the heart, wouldn't the bereaved say, *Don't you see how sad I'm feeling and how you and this dying shit hurts me?*

Sheer love and panic kept Annie at the bedside, but she hadn't wanted to see Mariel's relentless collapse. That was a fight no one in Vegas would put a bet on. What were the odds? What are the desert people in-the-know taking on beating the Big C? *I wasn't that horrid, was I, Mariel? Be semi-honest.* The odds weren't seductive enough to risk unconditional love. Dying people forget about their friends. They die cruelly, abruptly and they die forever.

The dead let us know how gone is gone.

"She is home with the angels." Annie was thinking about the euphemisms, what people think gives relief from such an abrupt finality. And isn't death abrupt, no matter how long it takes? *"She gone to her final reward"* – that heavenly home she and Mariel had joked about – the one with the condo and the indoor pool and the Sunday buffet to die for. *"She's with Jesus."* Lovely. Jesus liked her so much He killed her and took her ass with Him. No, no. Annie wouldn't be doing any of the Smiley Face Christian Bullet Points. Mariel was dead, simply, everlastingly dead. Devastatingly dead. She was *no* more. After a month or two a person probably couldn't separate the dirt from the bones.

Annie was still looking out the window.

A woman had just sat on a wood bench in the park – fifties, chunky, a white cape draped about her shoulders and arms. Sunshine flashed through the leaves and branches of the trees behind her. *Perhaps she's a nurse*, Annie thought. *Don't nurses wear capes? Or something religious, some type of nun*. The way many nuns dressed today only hinted at their calling, and every order dressed differently. Some wore a head covering, some not; some had capes, or skirts with a modest hemline, a person couldn't tell what was going on.

You don't fool me, pumpkin. Annie imagined she could hear Mariel, that amused, sarcastic tone. Smug, actually. And *so* John Lennon. *You don't believe any of that.*

"Why not? It could be true," she said to herself, looking down at the park.

No, it couldn't. You just want it to be true.

Annie watched the woman in the cape. Last night she'd read about another woman who had worn a white cape, this one in the Grendel diary. The woman on the wood bench raised her head and looked back at Annie.

You just want the world to shuffle along.

WHAT THE DIARY had done last night was to bring back an old dream that had repeated itself over the years as if it owned her. Or maybe she had blamed the diary for doing it. In the dream Annie was fifteen years old again and the night air was so very cold. A mist clung to everything – her clothes, her face – and she didn't know how to dry off and get warm. Annie thought she'd never be dry and warm again. The spaceship had felt that way, frigid and damp, it went through her skin, it made her bones sore. *I'm back on the ship. Oh shit. Oh Jesus. I'm back on this ship with the gray bitches. I've gotta get home. Daddy, help me, please. Where are you?* Annie thought Dr. Penske had also appeared in her dream – sort of a baldheaded middle-aged muscle boy, perverse but cute. He always smelled like one of those perfume ads you scratched and sniffed in

Vogue. Too sweet, *pheew.* He kept telling her she had PTSD.

"You know what that is?" he said.

"What people get after a war."

"That's right. Very good, excellent." At first Annie didn't see him; she only smelled and heard him. "That's what people used to called it," he told her. "Nervous From the Service. But the ones who called it that had no idea what it was like to have people wanting to hurt you, people who didn't know you and didn't want to know you. These people had their own ideas about you and they were happy to keep it that way."

"I got PTSD from fighting aliens," she'd whispered.

"There you go," Dr. Penske said.

"I'm Nervous From the Service."

Annie remembered hearing him grin, the crispy little popping noise the lips make when the skin separates for a smile.

Nervous from the intergalactic service.

She remembered other sounds. They came from deep inside the spaceship. Annie was on her back in the cold and the darkness. Maybe it was an operating room – *no, not that sort of room.* She heard water dripping against a metal floor. Everything smelled like copper and wet wool. *Water doesn't leak in an operating room, does it? A stinky old room like where they'd do abortions or something, that's what it felt like.* But Annie had no ideas what an abortion felt like. Her legs and arms were spread wide and secured with Duct tape. She'd been naked, her back on a hard surface, the chill of it brought fire to her skin, but after a while Annie's skin had no feeling. That was when Mariel had begun to scream. Far off and without direction – above, below, down, right or left – but definitely her, *I can tell a person's voice, even a person's scream.* Or perhaps just Annie had screamed and she'd imagined Mariel doing it, too. Drunken girls lost in a spaceship, jabbed in this hole and that, hearing them taking bets – *did Grays do that?*

"Bet I can fuck 'em both." The intergalactic bravado of three aliens? For the longest time, Annie thought so. *"Bust out her teeth so we can fuck her mouth."*

"Forget her mouth," one gray said.

"How many holes do you need?" another one said.

This was the moment when Grendel's woman in the white cape had appeared in her dream. A second or two before Annie opened her eyes, she'd heard the woman say to the Grays, "You can't have her, boys. Not anymore, not ever. Don't go feeling bad, but this one is mine. C'mon, give granny a big, big kiss."

"– READ ME THE *book.*" Beth Lee had become very frustrated and sounded either weary or drunk, Annie couldn't decide. The girl held onto the small wood table next to the window with both hands. The diary laid on the table and she softly batted her forehead twice against its leather cover. "I won't get scared if you're here. I promise, I *prom*ise." Tap. Tap.

"It's not for children. And stop that. You'll give yourself a headache."

Annie said this as gentle and polite as she could manage. *You just turned down a little girl with cancer. Who does that?*

"– Just a little, a *page*. A *page*." Beth was down to bargaining.

"I have to finish this," Annie said and nodded to the Grendel painting in front of her. "Your mom should be here *very* soon."

Five or so minutes ago Annie had gotten a call from the information desk. Mrs. Heather Latterimer was coming up to the conservation studio to get her child. Beth Lee had grinned and squealed when she heard the news.

The girl was tracing the burned letters LUC on the tan leather cover of the diary with two fingers, whispering each letter to herself.

"– What's it about," the child finally said.

At least tell her that. Quick and simple, that's all. I couldn't forgive myself if I didn't do something for this kid.

Mariel used to wear a t-shirt that said, *Spoil me, I have cancer*. Annie did, too; whatever Mariel wanted Mariel got. No ifs, ands or buts – no shit. "You think it, you got it." Not that Annie actually said those words out loud. It was unspoken but Annie used her credit cards and a loan or two from Big Ben Silva's bank account. Mariel knew she had to be careful about what she said. The two of them had lived a month in Athens thanks to a TV travel show and Mariel drinking a glass and a half of white wine: from that came the dreamy word *Greece*. Sharing her daydreams always got results.

That was how much Annie had loved Mariel.

–Quick and simple.

"Okay, fine." Annie leaned back in her mahogany swivel chair, her paint brush held between the thumb and middle finger. "Mr. Grendel's diary is about how he came to paint this landscape – *Meeting on the Steps to Hades*." Annie pointed the tip of her paint brush at the picture, the demons, the gold doors near the cobblestone steps. "It's also what happened to him *after* he painted it." Annie hesitated, arranging her thoughts then smiled to herself. "Most important, it's a love story. Scary maybe, but a love story. Mr. Grendel says they loved each other deeply – him and a woman in a white cape – and he writes how the woman took him into her dream."

"You *can't* do that," Beth Lee said, frowning.

"Not so, according to Mr. Grendel. He says that's where he got the picture." Annie looked out the window at the park across the street. "He says he stole it from the woman's dream."

5

The Plaza Mayor and Beth Yaacov Synagogue
Madrid

Thoughts on Luc Grendel

HER APARTMENT WAS on the fourth floor of the Plaza Mayor, an enormous rectangular building with balconies, dormers and angled slate roofs. Mrs. Grendel's balcony overlooked a 17th-century square where the Inquisition had tried and executed heretics. This was done to impress the faith upon the newly converted, mostly Jews and Muslims. Liesbet liked to sit on the balcony in the evening and have her *carajillo*, a coffee with brandy, the rim of her warm glass coated in sugar. She also liked watching the tourists – Mr. and Mrs. *Puto-Puta* – and the sky changing its color. Red and orange cluttered the beginning of the evening. Later long tracts of pink appeared against a new night. The sky was magnificent, the tourist less so. Seldom did she think about the Jews and the Muslims.

That wasn't totally accurate, Annie Silva was a Jew. Mrs. Grendel thought a lot about Annie. An artistic type – a romantic, no doubt, a sentimentalist who didn't grasp the indifference of things – what could you do? The girl was an emotional catastrophe, falling apart at the death of a friend she didn't have to acquire. What fool does that, who in their sensible minds choses to put themselves in such a position?

Annie friend had the worst end of it. Who'd dare love an individual tossed by her own currents? Oh, yes, Liesbet knew about artist types. They were thieves in every way a thief could be a thief. An artist never asked permission, artists stole indiscriminately. That was true, they took whatever they wanted whenever they wanted it. It was madness to love an artist, to get tangled in their words and in their eyes, to discover you are just another thing they have stolen.

NORTHWEST OF THE Museo de Prado was Beth Yaacov Synagogue. This evening Annie Silva had placed the Grendel diary inside her black leather handbag and wandered into the Comunidad Judia de Madrid, a neighborhood of narrow streets, tall ancient trees and clipped shrubs. She'd ended her walk at the synagogue but without planning it, not a clue about what was in front of her. Beth Yaacov had the look of a gray concrete parking garage. But the interior was nothing like the outside. Both the pews and the ceiling were polished tan wood, and the recessed ceiling lights were bright enough to wash out the flaws.

Beth Yaacov felt safer here than her apartment or the Prado. Big Ben liked to say a Jew could step into *shul* anywhere in the world and feel its embrace. "–It's like being home," he'd say. Her father was also the one who called it a *shul*, the German for school or synagogue.

"You goin' to *shul* this morning, kiddo?" He would stand by her bed, giving her toes a shake. Ben was usually ready to go at eight, dressed in his jeans, an old navy-blue corduroy sportscoat, and some cockamamie tie you couldn't figure. His favorite tie was bright yellow and had pictures of Elmer Fudd chasing Bugs Bunny. "Hey you, c'mon, go with the old man." Occasionally he'd sit on the edge of her bed and pretend his fingertip was a fly trying to get into her ear. "Let's you and me do a little Saturday *davening*, what you say?" *Davening* – from the Hebrew *Dovaiv*, to move the lips, to pray. Annie in any synagogue was always the nearest thing to being with her sweet Big Ben.

She picked the back row to sit and read, feet tucked beneath her, the leather-bound diary on her lap. Annie took a breath and let it loose, a soft audible sound. *Just relax, for godsake. Luc Grendel was just a depressed guy who drank too much. What's new?* She had read a couple of pages the night before last but decided to start from the beginning. To read it without her glass of red and Mariel's picture looming over her. Mariel hated this stuff – demons, fire and brimstone preachers, horror movies, anything or anyone who wallowed in the dark. "It doesn't matter if it's true or not," Mariel would say. "Why infect yourself with that shit? It's what you believe that'll get you crazy."

ROESELARE, WEST FLANDERS
Zomer, 1567

I am Luc Grendel, and I know where the demons live. I have started to dream them. I feel the creatures at the night while I sleep beside Liesbet, my new wife. Their breaths a wet ash and earth smell, their touch unintentional, thready. Liesbet and I have been married a month now. My beautiful bride, what more could I hope for? I've watched her smile when she is asleep and I cannot help wondering what sort of dream has caused it – me with a touch of jealousy, if I'm honest. Why should Liesbet's dreams give her a smile while my recent ones bring me nothing but a dark and abiding fear?

The first demon to haunt my sleep had stood outside my window in the moonlight and the snow. Its wings were translucent like long shadows, the wings a mix of bone and skin that ended an inch or two above the ground. People had walked by the demon as though it wasn't there.

Maybe only I can see this creature, that was my thought. I've finally become a drunkard like my father, my second thought. Am I doing what he did, seeing what no one else can see, yelling at invisible foes? It's become a constant worry since my marriage, though not enough to curb a bad habit. Rum for rum, fantasy for fantasy, I think I am chasing my father into hell. Or so says my conscience, what's left of it. And here I am, just married. God help my dear sweet Liesbet. Will I also take a fist to her for looking at me in too dim a light (or smiling in her sleep)? Will I someday stumble home and beat the children?

I would rather end my life than become my father.

I did not know why others hadn't given the first demon any attention. I didn't know I was dreaming. I remember seeing an older man in a tattered dark green coat walk through this demon and not a blink. He was oblivious to it, I am sure. Perhaps the demon didn't exist for him or for the others.

The second dream had a demon standing by the fireplace in my living room. Red coals and a haze of black smoke from the fire had outlined it. A female, I'm positive. It was muscular and low to the ground, yet a pleasant face, even a pretty face.

More importantly, it reminded me of Liesbet.

What are you doing here? I remember thinking but I kept quiet.

"Tell me you love me," the demon whispered. Though now when I think on it, I believe it must have been Liesbet, or a form of her. It sounded like something between a thought and a voice. But inside of me, my thought, my voice. "I can come into your dreams if you say the words," it said. Then the demon or Liesbet - whoever it was - said again, "Tell me, Luc. Say you love me."

"If you be Liesbet, it's true," I said. "I love you very much."

Why would I say such a thing? you might say. Tell a demon that I lcved it. In my defense, I ended up feeling this was not a demon but my wife trying to reach me through my dreams.

THE NIGHT HAD taken the last of the pink sky and had brought the stars and the cool air. Mrs. Grendel had another sip of the *carajillo* from a fourth-floor balcony in the Plaza Mayor. Yellow lights from the archways and the apartments gave her a view of the square below. Outdoor cafes, the *terrazas,* with their white chairs and red table cloths were scattered about its edges. *This was where the guardians of the church had tried and tortured the unfaithful*, Mrs. Grendel thought. *Now tourists in hiking boots and baseball caps take pictures with their phones and have wine and tapas*. Some younger people were sitting on the wore gray brick in small groups and talking. *Delightful. Forgive and forget.*

A very old conversation entered her mind – more in line with *not* forgiving and *not* forgetting – but she didn't know the year of it. She did better with associations than with time. If a person wanted to know what were some of the events that occurred in, say, 1842, Mrs. Grendel would be at a lost. But if you got specific and asked what she was doing when Giuseppe Verdi's opera *Nabucco* premiered in Milan – Mrs. Grendel being an opera enthusiast – she'd tell you about owning a café in Delft, a city 53.1 kilometers southwest of Amsterdam.

The conversation she had just remembered went like this:

"I ask your forgiveness," the man had said, her painter.

"Since when do you *ask* for anything?" Nothing was more amusing than a bewildered man. "Who needs permission for such things?"

"*Every*one."

Not a bad painter, really, if Liesbet thought about it. She'd said that more than once. His face came to her as she thought the question – so many years – sketchy but recognizable, the defined cheekbones, the pale green eyes, all that brown hair he tied-off and hanging to the middle of his back. His hair was always speckled with whatever paint he was using at the moment.

How does one ever forget my painter?

Her one and only darling, they were like an uneasy melody with too many violins, or she remembered it that way – her failing, her misstep, Luc Grendel. This was what her detractors pointed to, her "unnatural relationship," what they called it. "You married – *married*? Where was your judgment?" Eye rolling, sighs, what moronic shit detractors love to do. "How could you? What were you *think*ing?" *Like these Holier-Than-Thous never confused their ass with their elbow. How can they stand to live with their* *perfect selves?* The detractors forever pointed to her marriage as evidence of the cat getting too chummy with the mouse. "We told you. Didn't we do that, didn't we *tell* you?" This was what happened when one got to know the target.

Luc Grendel's last conversation with her hadn't gone well. They were in the cabin eating breakfast. The stone fireplace had a kettle for tea, and there was the smell of bacon and hot fresh bread.

"People forgive one another all the time," he said. "I would've forgiven you."

"Then you'd be a fool. You stole from me. I saw the painting in the shed." Her voice was calm and even, and she took a quick sip of her tea. "You think a tarp over it would keep me from noticing? What you painted belongs to me."

"If I painted one of your apples, the apple is still yours," he said, a not too subtle exasperation. "But the painting of that apple is mine."

"This is *not* an apple."

"Women understand nothing."

In those days she had loved Luc Grendel enough to let him into her dreams. "Lay here," Liesbet had said – this two or three days after they were married – and patted the bed next to her. She had used a rose-colored scarf to bond his wrist to hers and told him, "This is so you won't drift."

"What if I don't want a scarf?"

"I *need* to protect you."

"That's my job, isn't it?" He had that smile men get when women unintentionally amuse them. "I'm the man. I protect."

Fine. So no scarf.

When Liesbet was a young woman, she'd decided nobody but men could talk to men. Men did not listen to women. They knew everything and they wanted you to know they knew everything, and they also wanted to teach you everything they knew. Men have always seen themselves as the teachers of women.

"I thought it wouldn't matter." Luc had said this the next morning while Liesbet cleaned his left calf and bandaged it.

"You don't listen."

"It's *not* what the world does," he said. His tone was indignant, as if telling God, *How dare you do that.*

"There are worlds other than this one."

"– It's witchery."

"Oh much worse than that, dear husband."

In the dream Liesbet and her husband had paused on the stairway next to one of the gold doors. There were many stars and a half moon carved into the gold. The air had a stink to it. Luc said the odor reminded him of a barn that had accumulated the shit and piss of many animals. A small demon had come to him from behind and raked its claw down his left leg. The attack was very fast and Luc didn't notice it at first. As the pain grew, it burned like flesh held to a fire. He'd brought the wound back from their dream, back from one world and into the next.

THE BIG WINDOWS of Beth Yaacov Synagogue were stained glass and had the silhouettes of many flying birds –frightened birds or worse, a mass bird hysteria. Annie was still sitting in the last pew, the Grendel diary spread on her lap. For the last five or so minutes she'd been looking at the franticness of the windows and imagining the sound of all those wings. She remembered one of Mariel's poems, too.

You are in such a rush,
getting safe,
out of the way.

How do you see the storms before I do?

Annie looked down at the opened diary and tried to concentrate.

WOENSDAG, 1567

Liesbet stole my painting from the shed. I have no proof that she stole it but this is what I believe. Who else would do such a thing, or care? Perhaps it was the demon itself, the one who clawed me. If the world is like Liesbet says - a Russian doll with worlds inside worlds - it could be anyone or anything. I may have offended more than just my bride.

Who knows the demons who are after me now? My God I hate dwelling on the thought.

Liesbet will not sleep with me anymore. She sleeps on the dirt floor beside our bed. I tell her, "You are my wife. A wife must sleep with her husband." I am sure that is a law of some sort. If not a law, it should be.

This does no good, of course. She just turns her back to me and pretends she is asleep. My friend Obert says I should beat her, but I am not that type of man. I do not think a husband beating his wife will help her love him.

Yesterday I confronted Liesbet.

"My painting is missing," I told her.

Vegetables and potatoes were cooking in an iron pot that hung low in our fireplace. Liesbet was stirring the pot with a long-handled spoon I had carved for her last winter from the branch of a spruce.

"Perhaps I stole it," She said and began adding chunks of reindeer meat to her stew. "That's what you're saying, isn't it? Your wife stole your painting? Your beloved Liesbet?"

"- Well did you?"

"It's you who stole from me." She looked in my direction, no more than a moment, and returned to the pot. I thought I'd seen a smile. "I share my life with you and you think it is yours," Liesbet said, tossing in another piece of the meat. "And when I take my life back, you think I'm a thief. You need to look at yourself husband. You need to think about who is the thief."

"But did you do that?" My voice had a tremble in it. "Did you steal my painting?"

"You're afraid of me now."

She was right. A woman who could dream those types of dreams was not a woman who could be trusted. I also thought on what she said, that I stole her life, and I am not so sure what I dreamt with her was a dream. I look down at the bandage on my leg. Dreams do not do that. There are no dreams that can cut you and get you to bleed. This is not what dreams do, not any dream I know or have ever had.

Liesbet and I married without either of us knowing very much about the other one. I was so taken by her - and she by me, I think. I hear it is like that with some people. I knew she came from a town not too far from Amsterdam but I could not tell you the name of the town and I know nothing of her family.

She had not talked about her family, no talk I remember. The more I think on it the more I suspect I made up her younger life. An orphan, I'd thought. I saw her as one of many parentless children who wander our world and survived in ways that I preferred not to imagine. Or worse, if I allowed my fantasies to wander. I imagined Liesbet never being a child. I imagined her entering this world fully grown.

NINE-THIRTY OR so at night and the tourists hadn't quit the square at Plaza Mayor. Shadows and yellow light flickered beneath the *Arco de Chuchilleros*, people forever passing under the main archway, getting their fill and leaving. Mrs. Grendel found it uncomfortable and didn't know why. She was obsessed by the families and the whiny children and the young people making one another laugh. That was when a memory of another time in Madrid occurred to her – a restaurant near this square. She didn't recall the name of the restaurant but knew the name of the waiter. Salvino. He had dark curls about his ears and forehead and wisps of black hair on his chin. So thin a man she could have – but didn't, *never* would – circled her thumb and finger around his wrist. Salvino enjoyed performing American accents for his customers, Brooklyn, New England, Texas, Louisiana, each a perfect creation. She despaired at the way everyone found one another so amusing. It saddened and annoyed, it left her feeling like an orphan with her nose pressed against the glass store front of a bakery. Mr. and Mrs. Puto-Puta and their little Puto-Putas. They belonged to the same club and shared a mutual amusement. She belonged to no club at all.

Did you take my painting, Liesbet?

Did he have to ask?

Yes, she did; took the painting and his diary – his precious diary, his secrets for her secrets – and she refused to tell Luc any of it. Why should her husband be treated with any more respect than he'd given to her?

I wanted you to see my world and what did you do? You stole it and were about to show it anyone who'd look. Worse. Oh so much worse. You were ready to sell it to the highest bidder. But it's my fault, isn't, Luc? My weakness. I was so hungry and blinded by my love, any thought of betrayal left me.

And yet ...

Even when Luc Grendel was gone from her life, Liesbet could not destroy his diary or the painting. These feelings hadn't been lost on her, what love could do. Years later she would look back on that day and remember it each time others gave her the usual warning about her weakness.

– *Flesh and history will complicate your life. Better to keep the target down range and impersonal.*

But nothing is perfect, nothing and no one.

Liesbet could not bring herself to set these damning and intrusive things on fire. Instead she had wrapped the painting and the diary in oil cloth and tied them with hemp and sealed the cloth with wax made from deer fat. Soon it became time for her rest, an unstoppable, cyclical event – what she jokingly called "my little deaths" – and she had carried the package with her into a cave near Maastricht in the Netherlands, roughly forty kilometers from their cabin in West Flanders. Liesbet had to travel a quarter mile into the cave, where it was heated and the rock had holes that hiss and sprayed. Steam came from the holes like a trail of cigarette smoke and the smoke covered the area. The ground was muddy and very hot and smelled of feces, bats probably. Wet limestone dripped from stalactites and struck the calcified rocks below. She'd buried the package a few yards to the north of her resting place. Then the weariness enfolded her as always. Liesbet could not remember a time when it hadn't crept over her. She began digging a sleeping place for herself, what felt like hours. The lengths of her "little deaths" varied. They had a circadian quality but much, much longer – no thirteen or seventeen-year cycle for her. The shortest time was seventy-four years, the longest was close to a century and a half. When she awoke this particular time, the year was 1894 and the package she had buried was gone. Liesbet had to track her husband's painting and his diary through two more cycles.

6

Dr. Zeke Frieder's Office
Carmel, California

Winifred getting her bitches straight

"– KILL HER." DIDN'T Boring Eddy say that? *"You kill her, you get the bitch out of the way. Very simple, really."*

Late afternoon sunlight came through the open window in Dr. Frieder's office and across the pine polyurethane floor. The light was a brilliant splash of warn orange-yellow on the lacquered wall to Winifred "Freddie" Bane's left.

Which bitch was he discussing? She'd been churning about this for a week now. At the start Fred had thought, *Am I the bitch? Are they going to kill me?* She wouldn't rule out anything when it came to her asshole husband. *Haven't I been a good wife to you, Taylor? Let you bully me around, put up with your tantrums?*

"So what are you thinking?" Dr. Frieder said. Today the psychologist looked particularly disheveled, the left point of his denim collar pressed upward against a gray tweed lapel, his hair refusing the brush. He and Mrs. Bane were sitting in identical tan velour high-backs, opposite each other, a narrow wood coffee table between them. "I know you're used to keeping your thoughts to yourself," he said. "But that sort of thing doesn't work in therapy."

"Nothing to say." She forced a smile. "It's not important."

"Why don't you and I decide that together."

Freddie looked out the window at a cloudless sky and Carmel Bay. A keeling white catamaran raced and bobbed in sunshine.

"My husband is a calculating man, Dr. Frieder. Him and his two cohorts." Her hands were folded tightly in her lap, each grasping the other, the skin white from pressed fingers. As Fred looked down, strands of her red hair fell away from their combed and sprayed place and hung in threads about the sides of her face. She took a breath and tried to relax everything. Then she said, "I thought they wanted to kill me."

"Your husband?" The psychologist studied her for a second or two; saw a tremor in her left hand. "Is that what you're saying? You thought your husband wanted to kill you?"

"The three of them."

"You don't believe it, anymore?"

"I believe they want to kill *some*body, just not Yours Truly. Not that they'd do it, personally, either. They're way too chicken for that. They'll get it done, though, very neatly, quietly. No muss, no fuss, as the saying goes." She crossed her long legs at the knee and began clicking a black high heel off and on the back of her foot. "A couple sessions ago you told me to wake up. Well, let me tell you, what I heard this week did the trick."

"What will you do?"

"I already did it. I called the woman this morning."

"The one you think they're going to kill?"

"I told her she needed the police. I told her she needed to do something." Fred was looking down at the leg crossed over her knee. "It bothered me all last night, what I'd heard from my husband and those other two. A person overhears things, you know. I literally called Spain at eight in the morning." She absently ran a thumb and index finger along the crease of her jeans as she talked. "That's where this woman lives – Madrid, Spain. Can you imagine? There I am, talking to a woman I've never met. Telling her, basically, she was in *very* deep shit."

"What did the woman say?"

"Oh she thought so, too."

"– I KNOW THAT sounds dramatic." Mrs. Bane had just told Annie that a woman had been hired to go to Madrid and kill her.

Annie looked at the phone as if the thing was being dramatic on its own. She'd finished working on the Grendel painting for the day and was cleaning her last brush, thinking about what café on the Calle Ruiz de Alarcon served the best tapas. She placed the receiver to her ear again. "– Who *is* this?"

"The person who's going to save your life, sweetie."

"How did you get my number?" What Annie truly wanted to say was, *How the hell do you know about me and my life?* Or the usual *Go fuck yourself* and end it there, what Mariel would surely do – and did do, *liked* to do, in a heartbeat. But the thought that Annie's life actually needed saving brought a quick mix of shock and fears. "I'm hanging up now."

"Wait. Please. I'm a friend. No, a con*cerned* person. More that, really – a *very* concerned person." The woman had a slight panic to her voice. She paused and took an audible breath. "Listen to me, Annie. What if I said I found your name in my husband's book?"

"Then I'd say don't worry. Not my persuasion."

"It isn't that sort of book."

Annie shut her eyes; rubbed the lids gently with her thumb and forefinger. "You got less than a minute."

"*It's* a Things To Do book. Understand? It's not the sort of book you want to be in, believe me." The woman was speaking calmly now but her voice had a too controlled feel to it. "People do this and that, Annie. Some regret what they do. Have done. When they can't change that part of their lives – make it better, I mean – people like that, they have to get rid of the troubling part altogether."

"I'm going to need a name."

"Something happened to you." The woman was again hesitant with her words. "When you were a teenager, you and your friend – you understand me now?"

"... Taylor."

"Yes."

"You married Taylor *Bane*?"

"Yes."

"You can sure pick them, lady. Was it worth it?"

"Was what worth it?" The woman sounded lost.

"– All that money."

DR. FRIEDER NODDED toward Winifred Bane's hands. They were still folded on her lap. He gave a here-and-gone point of his finger. "What's got you shaking?" She gave him a puzzled look so the psychologist said again, "Your hands, can't you tell they're shaking?"

Fred squeezed her hands into fists as if to hid them from further critique. "I should never listen in on Taylor's conversations." She was scolding herself. Her black high heel pump hadn't stopped flicking up and down. “Believe me, the less I know about what’s going on with him, the safer I feel.”

“You did the right thing,” Dr. Frieder said. He was still sitting in his high-back chair, shoulders hunched, legs crossed. With his uncombed hair and wrinkled khakis, the doctor had the look of an unkempt Nome. “Warning her, this Annie person, that was a *good* thing you did. I’m sure it wasn’t easy.”

“Taylor doesn’t say much, you know. I read about the case – God, years back, the frat party, those two girls – awful stuff, *hor*rible – but when your family has money...” She dismissed the sentence with a little wave of her hand.

“– ‘When a family has money...’ what?”

Freddie looked at the psychologist, all expression washed from her face.

Dr. Frieder wasn’t doing to let this one pass. “Finish your sentence. ‘When a family has money...’ What? They can buy a big house? They can donate money to charities? Live in Paris. What? What happens when families have money?”

“Oh...you know.”

“Pretend I don’t.”

"They can keep their children out of trouble.”

“Okay, good. What do you think of that?”

“Life isn’t fair? I don’t know, sounds dumb when I say it.”

“– Not for people like the woman you called.”

Light from the window reflected the bits of dust in the air. Dr. Frieder’s office also had shadows in its corners now – the room dimming as the hour grew late – and there was an odor of stale pipe smoke.

“I didn’t put two and two together, not right away,” Mrs. Bane said, her voice soft, more to herself than anyone else. “I overheard one of Taylor’s friends tell him to ‘kill the bitch,’ that’s what he said. ‘Kill the bitch.' Like I said, I thought he was talking about me. But he was talking about Annie." *God, I wish I had a cigarette. Is there ever a perfect time to quit?* "When I don't want to see something, the thing could walk up and bite me on the ass – excuse the language – and I wouldn't notice 'til I looked in the mirror and saw the teeth marks."

"You're sure it's this Annie person?"

"Stop calling her that."

For a second or two the psychologist wasn't sure what he'd done.

"– Calling her 'this Annie person' all the time," Winifred Bane said. "Like the woman was a specimen in a jar, or whatever. Her name's Annie, just Annie."

Dr. Frieder didn't respond.

Fred took a breath, tried to steady herself. "Taylor has a book in his desk drawer. He calls it his To Do Book. I want you to know I've never gone through my husband's things. I feel ashamed of myself talking about this – this snooping. That's not what I do, not who I am. A snooper. *Je*sus. But I'm going through his mail – day after day, mind you – the pockets of his suits, his desk drawers, so on and so on. That's when I thought I was the bitch he was going to kill. One thing I did find in his book was a woman's name. Liesbet Grendel. It's Dutch, isn't it?"

"Do you know who she is?"

"I've heard Taylor and his friends talk about her."

"– And?"

"She kills people for money."

"DO YOU KNOW what they did with me and my friend?" Annie was sill on the phone with the Bane woman – what's-her-name, *Fred*. Like Wini*fred* or something. 5:47 PM and Annie had yet to leave the Prado. The phone had caught her just as she was going to the door. *Meeting on the Steps to Hades* was already draped, her brushes cleaned and on the portable work table. She needed to leave and quiet her growling stomach with some good tapas and wine.

"I remember the newspapers, the TV," Freddie said. "They showed school pictures of you and the other girl. The other one, what was her name?"

"– Mariel."

"Yes, Mariel. That big smile and all those shiny braces."

"You might have noticed how they didn't mention the boys. The press, I mean. They didn't mention the fraternity, the school, nothing." Annie felt herself getting pissed again. *Amazing how anger can shorten the years.* "– Just us, Mariel and me raped and beaten, and by who knows what or who – *whom* – im*mac*ulate destruction, invisible bad guys. Or maybe we beat ourselves up, you know how us girls are. Our sense of drama and all that. The school and your husband got more privacy than we did."

"So what's new?" Freddie said. "You ask why I'm with him, why I stay? You're right. I like being on the side of money. Money protects, it grants wishes."

"I've changed my mind about you. I don't think it's that – your money thing." Annie was looking out window. Trees along the avenue were filled with a fading orange sunlight. The last of the day went through the branches and the leaves, it speckled the sidewalk. Evening traffic crept along the Calle Ruiz de Alarcon. Annie shifted the receiver to her other ear. "You're scared," she said. "I'd be, too. If you left him, there would be no place to hide. If you left him, your name would be in that book. His To Do book, isn't that what you call it? That's what scares you, isn't it? What keeps you with him? It's not the money, it's the possibility of your name being written in that book, his stupid list."

"– Liesbet Grendel." Fred whispered. The name came out muffled. Annie thought the woman was talking too close to the phone.

"– *What*?" There was static on the line, too. Annie could barely hear. "You have to talk louder."

"The woman who has been hired to kill you," Winifred Bane said, but she was afraid say it any louder, afraid she'd be overheard. "Her name is *Grendel.* Okay? Can you hear that? *Liesbet* Grendel."

"You mean like the painter?"

"I don't know painters. I'm say it's *Gren*del."

"There's a painter named Grendel," Annie was shouting into the phone. Is the name like *that* Grendel?"

There was a dull electronic tone on the other end of line. The woman had hung up.

"I'VE DONE EVERYTHING I can do," Mrs. Bane said. The afternoon had become cloudy and there were more shadows in the room. She'd been looking down at her folded hands, afraid of Dr. Frieder's verdict on what she just said.

"What about protecting others?" He wanted to know.

"I knew you'd say that."

"But what would prevent your husband from doing this again – killing again? To others. To you. Let me repeat that, to *you.*" The psychologist was hunched over looking at her, slender hands linked about his crossed knee. "It's not that he may kill

Annie or have her killed. It's that he's killing."

"I've done what I can do, I think."

"I'm not saying you haven't helped her. You have, no question." Frieder looked at the round brass clock on the wall to his left. The session was almost over, two or three minutes, and he liked ending on time. "I'm saying your husband could get comfortable doing this, hiring thugs to solve his problems. And why not? He can do it at a distance. He doesn't have to know when or how. Forgive me but that's far too tempting for a man like Bane. You need to think this through."

"Maybe you more than myself," Fred told him. "Think of the implications. For me. Imagine what he'd do to me."

"I know the risks, I understand."

"Do you? I don't think you do." *How wonderful to be so cavalier with another person's life. Did they teach you that in school – how to know better than I do about my life?* "I don't think you understand anything."

"The police can be discrete."

"Good. Let them be discrete with your life."

"I'd be anxious, too," Dr. Frieder said. He glanced at the clock again. "Don't think I wouldn't. The repercussions could be – well – profound. But I would have to go. What else could I do?"

"Then you truly are naïve."

"They can protect you."

"I'll be blunt. The police can't protect dick. Taylor likes to call me his 'smart girl.' You know why he calls me that? Because I *know* him, I know how he thinks. If Taylor sets his mind to it, no one could protect me from him. It's one thing to call up a woman in Madrid and tell her to watch her back. It's a whole other story to call the police where I live – where my *husband* and I live."

Dr. Frieder looked at the brass clock on the wall and nodded. By this time Mrs. Bane knew that nod and knew her session was done.

As the psychologist walked Winifred Bane to the door, he was saying, “After a while, your Taylor will feel okay about doing away with the ones who disagree with him. He may feel that way already. Mr. Bane was given the go ahead at a very young age. ‘You can get away with it,’ they probably said to him. ‘We are rich and we are different,’ they probably said, maybe not in words but in actions, in deeds.” Dr. Frieder opened the door for his patient. “If you don’t go to the police, I will have to report this myself.”

“You told me our sessions were confidential.”

“What can I say? Within limits.” He shrugged, his hands raised slightly, palms up. “Everything has limits. But if you were going to harm another person, and I knew that and did nothing about it, I would be a conspirator. Or you telling me how Taylor is going to have someone killed and you’re not going to let anyone know. I’d *have* to report that. No one can let these types of events pass without notice. Surely you see what must be done?”

7

Jardin Botanico
Madrid

Lunch in the garden

FR. RAFA WALKED into the conservation studio at lunch time. “I’ve a surprise for you,” he said. Annie didn’t need the friar or his surprise. She’d been thinking about her talk with Winifred – that was yesterday evening – and also this morning’s visit to the Policia Nacional on a small street off the Paseo del Prado. Anything to do with Taylor Bane should be taken seriously.

Inspector Jorge Delgado had met Annie in his office. The man was a heart attack yearning to break free, mid-forties, overweight by fifty pounds and a cigarette hooked in the corner of his mouth, his left eye fluttering from the rising smoke. He spoke English *very* slowly as if he thought she was the sort of woman who had difficulty with her own language.

“An individual must do something against the law,” the inspector told her. “For example, threaten you, harm you or a loved one, so on and so on. You understand?”

“I’m not an imbecile.”

Annie had wanted to give the inspector Liesbet Grendel’s name but she’d decided against it. *Maybe I got the name wrong. So much static on the line. And Two Grendels, for God-sake. How likely is that?*

"Americans. You are a sensitive people, yes?"

That was when she left Inspector Delgado's office.

Okay, maybe a little sensitive.

After Annie's experience with the Policia Nacional, she wasn't sure what to do and she felt utterly alone. The anxiety had stayed with her all morning.

Fr. Rafa wasn't going to leave the conservation studio. "C'mon, guess my surprise," he said, determined Annie play along. This was when Beth Lee peeked out from behind his legs.

Sunlight came through the skylights and the large open windows. White walls and cabinets reflected the light. Annie could barely see the two of them. The girl was running toward her, arms open. She wore a pale blue cotton skull cap and another sleeveless dress, this one a very bright orange. Annie got down on one knee and they embraced. Beth Lee clung to her. Such a skinny thing, she felt like sticks and warm skin.

"You remember our Mrs. Heather Latterimer?" There was sarcasm to the friar's voice. "She told me Beth has talked about nothing but you. Lucky you, yes? So *Heather* thought, why not lunch for you and the child, mommy's treat. She wants you and Beth to become in*sep*arable buddies. This m.o.t.h.e.r is – what do you call it? – freaking out?"

"That spells mother," Beth Lee said.

"– And far *too* bright."

Fr. Rafa gave an audible breath and walked from the room.

Annie had no trouble sympathizing with Heather Latterimer. The first month after Mariel got her diagnosis of ductal carcinoma – a cancer beginning in the tubes that move milk from the breast to the nipple –Annie had the urge to run away, too. She did not want to see the only person she'd ever loved wither down to bones. She did not want to see what she could not stop. Avoid Sodom and Gomorrah at all cost – her love turning into a pillar of salt. Better to flee her life and the slow annihilation of what had brought her joy. The pain was unbearable, sorrow on an infinite and blinding scale. *How can you do this, Mariel?* That was what she'd thought – embarrassing to think about it now. *You lie in our bed and rot in front of me. You lose your flesh, your hair, the color in your face. You're becoming a stranger, a little more each day. You don't even do me the courtesy to disappear.* God did she really think that? Oh yes. What can a person say? Desperate times bring desperate thoughts. *I'll show you, my inconsiderate darling. I will leave you before you leave me – gather my toys and go home. Goodbye, goodbye. Wherever home is, wherever I'm supposed to go. Where the fuck is that, what little blip on my GPS? Where's my home without you, Mariel? Tell me the direction, show me the coordinates.*

Big Ben Silva had given his daughter Gustaff Mordecai's book *The Day and the Night of Dreams.* "Go read this," he'd said. "Read the 'notions' part." People like Ben who have had a little therapy are like people who've finally quit smoking, they become insufferably amused by everyone one else – the unenlightened, the nicotined – so Annie believed at the time. Big Ben gave her a loud kiss on the forehead and hugged her with his hairy monster arms. "Do you feel this?" he whispered and squeezed again. "That's what you do, pal. To the 'notions.' You got to turn around and hug 'em. Hard as you can, hug it out."

He'd been talking about how to stop what scared his daughter in her waking life and in her dreams. That was what the book had said, what the Swiss analyst Gustaff

Mordecai said. He called the things that frightened us "notions." Dr. Mordecai was 81 years old when he wrote *Dreams* in 1957. "It was true then," Big Ben Silva told his daughter. "And it's still true. Some shit doesn't change. Trust your old man, okay? After all, we *do* invent our dreams. Since they come from us, we need to make nice, particularly the bad ones."

Two days later, maybe three, Annie had sat down and began painting the portrait of Mariel naked in their bed – her white skin, her bones, her breasts gone dry. Mariel did die, of course, no dream there. But everything else was up for grabs.

"I MISSED YOU," Beth Lee said and looked up and grinned. Her toothless front space had begun showing its replacement, a white tip embedded in pink gum.

"I missed you, too." Annie didn't hesitate and her own enthusiasm embarrassed her. *They can really tell, can't they, Mariel? You were right, I AM the sentimental one.* Annie gave Beth's hand a squeeze. "You and I are going to have ourselves a wonderful lunch, pal."

Pal? Really?

That was what Big Ben had called Annie since...well...since close to forever. Before her mother, the notorious Jean Lynn Silva – the maternally challenged and carefree fornicator – left husband and daughter to marry Buster Connor and his penis. Her father once referred to Buster's penis as "the *schlong* that launched a thousand heartaches."

"We're pals!" Beth Lee yelled but to no one in particular.

Annie put a finger to her lips. "This is our secret."

The girl shushed herself and repeated in a whisper, "...secret pals."

Meeting on the Steps to Hades

They'd gone into a small grocery on the Paseo del Prado and Annie had bought a baguette and some mahon cheese and two orange sodas. After that they made their way to the Jardin Botanico near the museum. The day was sunny and hot and there were no clouds in the sky. Sections of the Botanico were sculpted trees and shrubs –wild roses, peonies, cypress, raisin and pomegranate, trees and shrubs from five continents – all cut into shapes and mazes. Other sections had a more natural look, simple meadows and wooded areas. Annie loved how sweet and heady everything smelled.

Beth Lee had found two white stone steps under the shadow of a giant cypress tree and she wanted to have lunch there. Annie sat next to her and gave the child some bread and cheese and twisted opened the cap of her orange soda. The stone steps had been carved to fit around the tan root of the tree. Beth thought this was totally amazing and poked the root with her finger.

"The tree has toes," Beth Lee said.

"Roots, honey. They're called roots."

"– Tree toes."

Across the graveled pathway was a trimmed lawn with ancient shade trees and wood benches. People lay on the grass to get the sun or they sat under the trees to stay cool. Some were having their lunches, others just relaxed and talked. *This is nice*, Annie thought. A Fr. Rafa suggestion. *Maybe I've been too critical of the friar. He can be stuffy but let he or she who is without a flaw cast the first you-know-what.* People also sat on the wood benches, mostly older folks and a few business types in suits and very shiny shoes.

"That woman waved to me," Beth Lee said, her hand cupped to the side of her mouth as if the information was top secret.

"What woman?"

"There." The girl pointed beyond the gravel pathway. "That one."

"Hey no pointing."

The woman on the bench smiled and waved again. Annie had seen her a day or two ago in the little park opposite the Prado. Maybe fortyish – older, younger, an age a person couldn't pin it down – *that's how you're going to look in another ten or so years, comfortable shoes and chunky calves.* The woman wore a white cape that draped her, shoulders to knees.

LIESBET HAD MORE time than she wanted to contemplate. Occasionally it overwhelmed her to think about the many years that had passed and the many more that waited for her. This notion about time had come and gone while she sat under the long full branches of an oak and watched Annie Silva and the child. A sick child, that was obvious. Very pale, her small bones pressed tight against the skin. The girl wore a blue skull cap, probably hiding the ravage of her treatment. It always perplexed Liesbet, how these treatments were as devastating as the disease. Liesbet had waved to her. *No need to hurry,* that was always her sense of these moments. *It's like dance, isn't it? But only one partner can hear the music – knows the beat, so-to-speak.* She enjoyed this part of it, the plotting, the flirtations, ingratiating herself. The final look of surprise was always worth whatever scenario she had to invent, whatever company she'd been contracted to endure.

"Amusing yourself, are you?" her husband liked to say.

Grendel knew her from the start. None of Liesbet's tricks or schemes ever got to him. Never once had the man said, *How could I've been so fooled? What sort of monster are you?* As if there were different types: the bad, the very bad, the one who does this instead of that. Spits fire. Chews throats. Eats children. He knew what she was but he also knew what she kept from herself. Who doesn't want to be known and found not guilty?

"What are you up to, Liesbet?"

"Why must I be up to anything?"

"Because it's your nature."

"You know nothing about my nature."

"Keep thinking that, if you've the mind. That is your nature, too." Her husband was painting in the field behind their cabin, the first warm day of spring. He was always painting. Meadows. A cluster of trees. Wildflowers after a rain. Simple pictures from a simple man. Liesbet remembered his dark hair tied off, the tail of it ending at mid-back. Greasy hair with flecks of whatever color was on the brush, that's how unkempt Grendel would get on his painting spree. When Grendel painted, he became like a drunk who'd forget all but the bottle. "That will be your undoing," he warned her, meaning the tricks, the concealment. "People who think they're inscrutable can't help but show themselves."

"And what do I reveal, husband?"

"Your cruelty, usually."

"Cruelty is it?" She'd been very close to laughing but thought better of it. Being in love and holding back the monster could be humiliating. "My cruelty doesn't stop you from climbing onto me every night."

"What can I tell you? You're my perversion."

Luc Grendel had saved Liesbet, scooped her up gently, as if she were no more than kindling. That was how they met. *He's rescuing me.* She'd never been rescued in all her years. *How remarkable.* She had broken a couple of bones – her left leg, the upper part of her left arm. Cuts bloodied her face and clothes. Later Luc learned the town had gone after her – not the entire town but enough of them – the women more than the men. They said Liesbet had turned the people of the town against each other, child against parent, husband against wife, the old against the young. Each day a new trouble was added to the list. The failure of crops, an accidental fire, a young mother dying in childbirth, a week's rain that swelled the roads with enough mud to stop the wheels of wagons and carriages. If more than one person caught a cold or had a fever, the rumors would start again. "She's doing it to watch us suffer," one woman had said, far more than one. "Telling people this husband is cheating with that one. Getting the children sick. I've never seen anything like it." This proved what Luc Grendel had suspected. If a man or woman says something often enough, others will join in and soon everyone will begin to believe it.

The women of the town had stoned Liesbet. They'd trapped her in a small empty smokehouse, their skirts filled with stones gathered that morning. "Seemed like she let us do it," one said. And another added, "She stood there and smiled. Nobody gets hit with rocks and smiles, the fool was bleeding. I think the smile got us worked up. Getting that smile off her face became a challenge."

Liesbet thought Luc Grendel had fixed her cuts and bones well enough. She could have done the job on her own and healed herself. Her body would have done it.

The pain of receiving a wound had always felt real. She couldn't escape the agony but no wound lasted for very long – an hour, two at most. Liesbet did not understand how the healing occurred, only that it did. And thank the ruler of worlds, it did. This was her curse and her grace – the pain of the wound and the quickness of the healing. Where she came from there were bodies stacked in piles of fifty to a hundred deep. Many stacks, as far as a soul could see. The skeletons were charred and had the look of marionettes. Yet while minutes ticked on, she'd hear the pop and crinkle of growing muscle, tendon and flesh. When the new nerves appeared, the screaming began. Liesbet couldn't hear herself think. There were screams in the darkness, screams in the smoke and the light of distant orange fires.

It didn't matter that she would've healed on her own. No one had ever tended to her, that was the point. Luc Grendel and Luc alone had helped her. He'd seen to her wounds and cared for her. Liesbet was surprised how she'd longed for this concern, this bewildering, all-encompassing tenderness. The lust she felt for it embarrassed her. His service had touched her heart.

BETH LEE LEANED closer to Annie and whispered, "– It's that woman. She's walking over here."

"Uh-huh, I can see, pal."

"I don't like her."

"You don't know her," Annie whispered back. They were still eating their bread and cheese on the stone steps in the shade of the big cypress tree. She patted the girl thin bare arm. "Relax. You let me do the talking. Okay?"

"Do *you* like her?"

"Why don't we agree she's okay 'til she does something weird. Give her the benefit of the doubt, so-to-speak."

"– The what?"

"Let's wait to see if she's crazy."

Beth Lee brought her fingers to her lips to hide a smile.

Are you the woman in Taylor Bane's To Do Book? Are you the one whose name is written next to mine?

Liesbet Grendel – from the 16th century?

Jesus. They will take me back to the hospital, for sure.

But Annie imagined calling her "Liesbet" just to see the response.

Liesbet, my ... what was she, her assassin? Come on, shoot me or stab me or do whatever you do, Liesbet. It's too fucking lonely here, anyway. I miss Mariel so much I'm attaching myself to babies.

Annie had read about Taylor's red, white and true blue patriotic phase, the committee exploring his bid for the senate.

He would have to kill her.

Erase her from planet earth, every squeak and follicle of her. Erase her from this Milky Way, this universe and all the parallel universes in all the kinks of time and space. The would-be Senator Band already knew the questions they'd ask her.

Do you know the senator?

How do you know him?

Senator Bane could also guess Annie's answers all too well.

Oh yes, sure, I know Taylor. We go way back. He was one of three aliens who took my friend Mariel and me to their spaceship and raped us in every orifice they could fine and with everything they could find.

Senator Bane was a very bright man.

The woman in the white cape appeared in front of Annie and the girl too quickly, as if a section of time had been clipped and tossed. She'd gotten up from her bench and began walking through the sunshine, across the mowed lawn. Then snip: the woman was kneeling in front of the child, white cloak draped about her short muscular body. There was a scent of burnt cinnamon, perhaps her perfume. *How did you do that? Get here so fast?* Annie wondered if she hadn't blinked or turned away from the woman for a moment, an unthinking shift in attention, and it only *seemed* like a cut in time. Certainly it could have been that. How many times had Mariel or her father scolded her about not giving them her attention. *Did you hear me, Annie? Are you listening, or am I talking to myself? It's rude, you know, what you do.*

So certainly it could have been that.

Liesbet looked at Beth Lee. "How very pretty you are, dear."

"What do you say?" Annie said.

"Thank you."

"I can tell she's a sweet child." Liesbet touched the girl's face with her fingertips, tracing the outline of her cheek. Beth shut and opened her eyes like a cat whose fur was being stroked. Her body appeared to go loose and she leaned against Annie's shoulder.

Her eyes were closed now, and the woman continued to touch her cheek. "She's very sick, but you know that. You've seen it before, yes?"

"What've you done?"

"She needs to rest."

"You go on," Annie held the child, both arms around her. "You let us have our lunch in peace."

"– Or *what*?" Liesbet studied her, two, three seconds, maybe a bit longer. Then she turned and stared at the empty bench on the opposite side of the narrow gravel path. “What’ll you do if I give you no peace?”

“Get the police, I can do that.”

“Look around, tell me what you see?”

Sunlight covered everything and Annie had to squint, cupping her hand above her brow. Something was different but she didn’t know what, not immediately. The silence came first. Jardin Botanico had no sound – no birds, no children, even the traffic noise had quit. A moment later it came to Annie that she, Beth Lee and the woman wearing the white cape were the only ones in the garden. Nobody picnicked on the grass or sat on the benches or walked the graveled pathways. This always crowded place had emptied of life and sound. *What is happening to me?* The push of her heart got stronger in her ears and chest. *Don’t hurt this child. Please don’t do that.* Her usual surety had started to unravel, that sense of how the world works, the everydayness of things. Panic crept in: hot and cold at the same time. She tried to stand but her legs and hips wouldn’t work. Beth Lee still slept, cheek on Annie’s shoulder, fingers pressed deep into her left arm.

“– Just go ... please,” Annie said, a voice quiet but sure and firm.

Bits of the meeting with Inspector Delgado came to her, the cigarette smoke, his condescension. *I’ve been threatened now, fat man. Isn’t this a threat?*

“Helping another sick girl won’t bring the other sick girl back,” Liesbet said. She had a bit of a smile at the right corner of her mouth. “Mariel, wasn’t it?” No waiting for a reply. “It won’t bring Mariel back.”

“– You *stop* it.” Annie whispered.

“When I’m ready.”

8

In a Limo
Carmel, California

Mrs. Bane goes for a ride

"THIS ISN'T OUR LIMO," Winifred Bane said. She'd called her husband on her cell. Fred was in the backseat of the limo that wasn't hers, feeling uncomfortable and looking out the tinted window. The car sped down Cabrillo Highway, Carmel Bay to her right.

The night sky had stars and a moon big enough to shine on the water. "You know I don't like surprises."

"You love surprises," her husband said. He seemed preoccupied, his interests divided.

"Well not *weird* surprises."

"How long have we been married?"

"– Seems forever." Sometime shit just slips out.

"What day is today, Freddie?"

She thought about it. "Oh my God."

"– Nineteen years today."

"Oh my God."

"Happy anniversary, my darling."

"You are some guy, Mr. Bane."

"You're some gal, Mrs. Bane."

That was the thing they liked to do. As in, "How's the lovely Mrs. Bane doing this fine morning?" And she answering, "Just waiting for the exceptionally handsome

Mr. Bane to join me for breakfast." This always got a good laugh over their wheat toast, coffee – black for Mr. Bane; cream and two sugars for the Mrs. – and Cheerios with a sliced banana.

The car must have been going eighty, including turns, and Winifred did not feel a quiver or a shake. She could have been lounging in her bed with a Scotch-rocks and a good book. The night and the silky blackness of the bay fled by her. Stars cluttered the sky. The highway was empty, reserved for her.

"So what is it, Mr. Bane?" She giggled; let the little girl out and used her pouty voice, "What sort of a surprise did you get for your Freddie?"

"Well that wouldn't be a surprise then, would it?"

"You're such a tease. I can keep a secret." Ha, ha.

"Did you forget our anniversary?"

"Have I ever?" *God, I did forget. Where was my mind?*

"– On occasion, darling," he said.

Winifred Bane switched the phone to her other ear, looking at the sliding glass partition that separated her from the driver. Was it a strange new driver to go with the strange new limo? She couldn't see enough of him to know what was what.

"You're not the only one with a surprise," she said, half-coo, half-breathy.

Hopefully it sounded sexy and mysterious. *shit, shit, I got nothing. Think.*

"You forgot." The perceptive Mr. Bane.

"No, no. That was your last wife." Another, ha, ha. Freddie tried to come up with something. Anything. Then it occurred to her. "You know that sex stuff you keep hustling me to do?"

"What stuff?

"You know. That...*stuff.*"

"You're kidding."

"Shhh. What*ever*."

"You're serious." He sounded amused.

"Yeah. Tonight's your night, Tarzan."

"YOU'D DO THAT?" Mrs. Bane couldn't believe Dr. Frieder. At the end of her last therapy session, she had stood by the open office door, looking at the psychologist. "You would go to the police? Truly?"

"A person's life has been threatened," Dr. Frieder said, more serious than she'd ever heard him.

"Annie's in Ma*drid*, c'mon. I called her."

"The man who's going to have her killed – your husband – where is he? Where does he live?"

"You know where he lives."

"Pretend I don't. Where does your husband live?"

"– Okay, fine. Here."

"Uh-huh, exactly."

This morning the Monterey County Sheriff's Department called her cell phone, Deputy Alec Martinez. He told her she could come down on her own or he could send out an officer to drive her. Which would she prefer? *Oh I prefer my neighbors see me get into the back of a cop car. They don't have enough to talk about, these bitches.*

She'd glammed down for Martinez and the boys. Dark gray suit, sensible heels, minimum lipstick and eyeliner, tasteful gold earrings. No Jersey shit. Freddie had also thought about dying the red hair, maybe a subdued brown, but decided she wanted them to at least be a *little* interested.

"You, uh –" Deputy Martinez stood at the doorway to his office, staring at an opened manila folder. "– What's the name–Winifred?"

"Winifred Bane, yes."

The deputy nodded and walked back into his small office. "Have a seat, Mrs. Bane." He pointed to the wood chair next to his desk without looking at her.

Martinez was a short man, five-two, maybe three, with a thick neck and big arms, maybe a weightlifter. Winifred thought short guys were always trying to figure out how to offset the short thing. Like you were either six foot something or a punk wanting a butt fuck, nothing in the middle.

"It took a lot for me to come here," she said.

"I understand your husband threatened to kill somebody." He obviously did care that it took a lot for her to come there. "An Annie somebody." The deputy sat down at his mahogany desk and glanced at the manila folder again. "Annie Silva. Where is she now – Madrid? That's like what – Spain?"

"Exactly like it."

"A yes or no is good."

"Yes, deputy."

"Deputy Martinez."

"Okay, Deputy Martinez." *Save me from short men.*

Already this guy was an asshole. It didn't take long. That was the positive thing about assholes. A person could count on them. In five minutes you knew who they were and you knew it wasn't going to get any better than the first five minutes. All situations in life should be that simple. The wood chair by the desk was hard and uncomfortable.

"You give me courtesy, I give you courtesy," the deputy said. He was still looking at her folder.

"What a lovely office you have, Deputy Martinez." *Might as well try to get along*, she thought.

"Yeah, a real beauty." Martinez kept reading. "I got four cinderblock walls painted puke lime and a fluorescent light that hums."

"What does it hum?" Humor never hurt, either.

"Jerry Vale hits, what do I know?" Finally the deputy looked up at her. "Listen, if I want my balls busted, I'll stay at home with the missus. Though I should be fair. At least she does her, you know, wifely duties."

"Well what stays in Vegas."

Deputy Martinez stared at her, all expression had left him.

"It's a saying."

"You think you're smarter than me?" He stared at her.

"No, no," she said, shaking her. She even waved her hand "no" in case he didn't get it. *Shit, shit. Shoot yourself in the foot, why don't you. Jesus.* "Hey, I'm a complete imbecile, believe me. *I'm* the imbecile here. Me. You're looking at her, okay? I think my husband just keeps me around to amuse himself."

"The husband that's going to kill the woman?"

"Well that's another matter."

"But that *is* the husband that's going to kill this other woman?"

"– Yeah. That's him."

THE LIMO HAD traveled up the coastline, a much higher elevation now. The night had no clouds and the sky was filled with stars. Mrs. Bane looked down a slopping side of rock, trees and shrubs to see the water. She pressed one of the silver buttons on the console next to her. The tinted window lowered and the smell of the ocean rushed about the back of the car. "Hooray for planet earth," Winifred muttered, though to no one in particular. *How stunning, how remarkable*: its dark and silver water, its moonlit paths, its searing fragrance of pine and soil and quick soaking rain. If a person wanted to see the earth in all its glory, Big Sur was a very good place to start. *Thank you, Taylor. For putting me right here, right this second. This is my best anniversary gift ever. Thank you, thank you.*

Freddie knocked on the glass partition that separated the driver from the luxury and exclusivity of the backseat. There was no answer. She knocked again.

Isn't this *glo*rious!" Mrs. Bane shouted at the glass. Then she knocked one more time. "– Hello? Can you hear me? Do you see all this? Isn't it wonderful?" Getting no answer, she settled back against the gray leather seat and looked out the window. "Well I think it's wonderful," she whispered to herself. "It's the most wonderful thing."

Winifred Bane called her husband again.

"I love you," she said.

"Who is this?"

"– *Tay*lor."

"I'm kidding, Freddie. I love you, too."

"Why aren't you here with me? We should be sharing this." She was looking out the open window, the cool air fluttering its dampness across her face. "You should see the moon, Taylor, how it is on the water. Like tiny gold coins. It's *so* beautiful."

"I'll get away as soon as I can, believe me."

"Get away now."

"There are people who don't care if it's our anniversary," her husband said. She thought he sounded frustrated by the whole thing. Or maybe she imagined it. Then he said, "People I have to talk to, *not* people I want to talk to. That's the story of my day. You'd be surprised how much of what I do is damage control."

"When will I see you?"

"– Soon."

"You're really missing out, you know."

"Such is my life, Freddie."

"But I *am* going to see you right?"

"– Of course."

"It's our anniversary, Taylor."

"I know. Lot of years, you and me."

"We have our moments, don't we?"

"– More than fingers and toes."

He sounded ...different; especially the last sentence. She thought her husband seemed melancholy. And that wasn't Taylor. Sarcasm was more his style. Even anger or being plain mean, that was his style, too. Sadness required self-reflection, didn't it? Nothing like, say, scheming; nothing like the daydream of becoming a senator, either. No, self-reflection wasn't Taylor's what-you-call-it, skill set, wasn't what the man did. She'd had enough therapy to know *genuine* self-reflection. A person needed to look inside his or her heart, or whatever. That's what Dr. Frieder had told her. That was *true* self-reflection. The real deal. We had to think about how we hurt others, or wanted to, or how others hurt us or wanted to. Not just say, "Oh, yeah, I remember that. Sure I do." But *really* think about it, think about it like you *mean* it.

Imagine Taylor doing that.

"ANYONE WILLING TO collaborate your story?" Deputy Martinez had said that morning. Winifred Bane sat on a wood chair next to the officer's desk. The small office had lime green cinderblock walls and two overhead florescent lights. One of the lights continued to blink and hum. The deputy was staring at Mrs. Bane's file rather than look at her as he talked. "Somebody reliable, good character, that sort of thing."

"You're saying my character isn't good enough?" Freddie felt anger heat her cheeks. Felt hurt, too. *Maybe I'm being too sensitive.*

"That's not my point."

"So what *is* your point?" A surprising edge to her question. *You really need to calm down.* She paused then released a tiny audible breath. "Officer Martinez –"

"– Deputy."

"Fine. *Deputy* Martinez. What are you asking me to do?"

"Nobody's committed a crime, Mrs. Bane."

"Does that mean we wait until somebody shoots her?"

"I'm not saying that, no –well not exactly that." The deputy's office didn't seem to have any ventilation and Martinez's short sleeve khaki shirt had dark wet marks under his arms. He had big, hairless arms. Fred thought it was an odd combination, maybe a Mexican thing. The deputy was saying, "...we in law enforcement don't arrest people before they do something, that's what I'm trying to convey here. Would you like being arrested before you committed a crime?" He didn't wait for her to answer. "I think not, Mrs. Bane. A shooting, a robbery, whatever it might be, the thing has to be committed *first* before we go in with guns blazing." Deputy Martinez stopped a moment to think about that last sentence and he said, "– Well, you know, not blazing, *per se*. But you get what I mean."

"Wait 'til the person's aiming the gun."

"Right. Pretty much, yeah."

MRS. BANE WAS sitting in the back the limo thinking about a list of restaurants and hotels in or near Big Sur that her husband might consider for their anniversary. She never had been good at guessing. Something with a view, of course. Elegant, of course. The man had many character flaws but elegance wasn't one of them. Taylor knew his romantic spots. That's one reason why he'd initially interested her – an elegant bad boy with money. What girl in her right mind didn't like that? Nice clothes, nice haircut, lots of attitude. Once a guy was talking sex stuff with her in this okay club in Monterey – her husband right there at the *table* – and she recalled how Taylor had looked over at Boring Eddy who was across the room, leaning against the bar and watching them. Next thing, Mr. Sex Mouth and Eddy were walking out of the club together. Sex Mouth attempted to struggle his way loose but got nowhere.

"What are they going to do?" She'd wanted to know.

Taylor had shrugged and grinned. "What people do, darling." He ordered her a gin and tonic, her favorite drink back then, and that was the end of the discussion.

Very gangster, very Taylor. Freddie liked it.

The Wave.

Yes, The Wave, that was Taylor's sort of restaurant. Now Freddie leaned her head on the soft gray leather of the limo's backseat and pressed the silver button on the console beside her. The tinted window closed and the wind and the ocean smell that had filled the car stopped. Taylor would take her to the Wave. Three stars or five stars, whatever it was, the cuisine tasted sublime. Freddie smiled to herself. They'd sit on the terrace and look down at the ocean. There were spotlights below – red and blue ones, mostly – and a person could see the waves hit the rocks and shatter like crystal.

The Wave, definitely.

Winifred Bane noticed the car had stopped, the side of the road near the ocean. The glass separating her from the driver lowered.

"How you doin' this fine night?" the man said.

"– Deputy Martinez?"

"Just Martinez. I'm off duty."

"You're my driver?"

"A man's got to make a living," Martinez said.

Part of him was in the shadow, his neck, the tops of his big shoulders. But Mrs. Bane saw the pistol and its silencer. Martinez fired two shots into her forehead.

9

Calle Ruiz de Alarcon
Madrid

Annie and Beth Lee have a sleep over

BETH LEE HAD gone to sleep immediately. Annie was sitting up in the bed reading Luc Grendel's diary – maybe not the best idea, considering the day–Beth's thin arm lay across her lap, the girl's mouth open, her breathing audible. Annie looked down at the child. *You were one tired little kid. The two of us, really – I'm worn myself.* But as tired as Annie was, no sleep had come. Busy Brain, her father liked to call it. "You got the Busy Brain, pal," he'd say. "You get it from me, you know. I once stayed up a week straight."

Afternoon lunch ended in a drama. Annie had scooped up Beth Lee with both arms and did a walking trot out the Jardin Botanico and away from the woman with the white cape. And what had the woman done? What terrible thing – talked longer than Annie thought appropriate, talked about taking care of Beth the way she took care of Mariel? That was a freak out – hearing Mariel's name -- but the woman could have been a friend of a friend. Mariel knew lots of people, they both did. There'd been no need to grab Beth and run. *God, I acted like a crazy person.* The woman was telling Beth that she had come to Madrid to see "all the lovely art" and mentioned the Museo De Prado, particularly the painting *Meeting on the Steps to Hades* that her great uncle had painted. No, her great, *great* uncle, a Flemish painter, but she was speaking to Annie through the child, or so Annie thought.

–Looking at Beth but speaking to me. Why not just talk to me? God it got too creepy. There was a wrongness to it that couldn't put my finger on. I think she knew I was restoring Luc Grendel's painting.

Still. The woman could have been Liesbet Grendel – probably was Liesbet. Funny how the mind goes dumb when a person is scared.

Not that I'd asked her. So stupid, so much a coward. Such a simple question, too. Annie had pictured herself saying, "*– So do you like Flemish painters? I'm working on one in particular. Have you ever heard of the picture Meeting on the Steps to Hades by Luc Grendel?*

A simple yes or no, please.

The strangeness didn't end there. When Annie and Beth Lee got back to Prado, Beth's mother was in the studio, waiting for them.

"– But she *wants* to sleep over." Heather Latterimer said. Heather had a crazed look. Her eyes literally vibrated when she talked, her words clumping together, as if she'd forgotten to take her lithium. Or maybe she was afraid Annie would poo-poo her idea before she got the thing out of her mouth. "Don't you, dear?" she'd said to her daughter. "Don't you want to sleep over? Tell, Miss Silva. Isn't that what you say to mommy?"

"You don't know me," Annie said.

"I trust Beth's judgment."

"She's five."

"No, no. Practically six."

There were days when a person could not escape crazy.

Mrs. Latterimer had long gold-blond hair set in stringy ringlets. Her hair showed the secret part of herself, the uncombed and fried part. She'd knelt in front of Beth Lee, fixing the strap on the orange sundress, fidgeting with the ends of Beth's hair that showed about the periphery of her cap. Heather's words rambled non-stop as she did it, "That's all the child talks about – well that, and how her bones hurt. It's the treatments, I think. God, I dunno."

"It's not that I don't understand," Annie said. She didn't want to look down at Beth Lee. She couldn't deal with those eyes. "I mean not ex*act*ly, I don't have children. But I lost somebody – recently lost somebody – so I know a little."

"No parent should have to watch their child go through this whatever, torture."

Heather was still kneeling in front of her daughter. She'd been rubbing a smudge from Beth right cheek with a white hankie. "Everything hurts her, poor thing. I just never know what to do."

"It's a helpless feeling. I get it, believe me."

Mrs. Latterimer glanced up at Annie. "She likes you. You know? I can let her spend time with you, I can do that much. Unbelievable, really. A suffering child – it's one of the great arguments against God, isn't it?"

THE SLEEPING CHILD now rested her head on Annie's lap, along with a limp outstretched arm. The small nightstand lamp was the only light in the bedroom, a yellow circle that illuminated the two of them. Annie had continued to read the Grendel diary while she stroked the bits of fine hair on Beth's warm scalp. When Mariel lost her hair from the treatment, had shaved her own head. Solidarity, Annie Ann it. Mariel had smiled and said, "– My c?nental Annie."

VRIJDAG, 1567

...Liesbet had appeared one afternoon in e field behind my cabin where

I painted. I looked up from my work and there she was, the sunlight behind her like some heavenly creature cloaked in white.

"I've seen you in the town," she'd said.

No woman had ever approached me before this one. I am a man who paints.

I do not drink. I do not whore. I don't go to church. What energy and time I have goes into my brush, my paint and canvas. It's why I was put on earth, I know nothing else. So I can easily turn into a self-conscious bumbler by the simplest attention.

"Do you need someone to pose for a painting?" she said. "The French and the Italians paint pictures of women."

"The Flemish also paint women." My sensibilities go prickly in the best of times but here I felt insulted. I imagined I'd been called a eunuch, or close to it – an ineffectual bit of meat – and now I had to defend my virility and the virility of all Flemish men. "You think the Flemish can't see the beauty of our women?"

"I didn't say that." The woman seemed embarrassed.

"But I'm certain that's what you meant."

She pressed two fingertips to her lips. "Then I've been quite imprecise.

Forgive me, I'm forever getting myself misunderstood. I should have said, the French and Italians know women."

This was not my imagination. "And e Flemish do not?"

She dismissed this with a flick of h hand. "I am in need of work," she said. "I name is Liesbet. The people in this tow won't give me work. I am looked upon with suspicion."

"The Flemish don't know women?" I couldn't help it.

"See? I've hurt your feelings, too. I cannot say what the Flemish know or don't know. I'm not from here. I've been in this town no more than a month and everyone is upset with me. I thought an artist would understand, accept my imperfections. It's a most peculiar place, this town. Perhaps it has to do with the dampness of the sea."

Liesbet became my model. What artist doesn't want to understand the woman who cannot be understood? It is one of many ways we torture ourselves.

I had always admired women who had some flesh on them. The old and the fat, these are the people artist's treasure - so many lines, so many lovely nooks and shadows. Not that Liesbet was fat, I don't want to imply that. She had a solid body. She had the beef of an earth goddess.

"That's not me," she'd say, looking at the progress of my painting.

"You are a beauty."

"I'm not that fat."

I told her she was what the Romans worshiped.

"My ass isn't that big."

"I thought you said the Romans knew women?"

"Yes, fat women. Haven't you seen their women?"

I do not mean to show Liesbet as critical or dissatisfied here. Part of her always understood the humor of life. There was that little smile on the rim of her words.

She was forever amused.

AND WHAT AM I supposed to do with you? Tell me that, you sweet thing; tell me, please. What are the rules? Annie had stopped reading Luc Grendel's diary. She was looking down at Beth Lee, the child's head resting in her lap, that thin arm drooping over the wrinkled sheet like a fallen twig. *Am I meant to relive Mariel's last days for my entire life? Is that how it's going to be? I don't mind being Beatle Paul, being sentimental. But I'm not a chump, as daddy likes to say.* Big Ben Silva loved words like "chump" and "pal" and "sport." He'd say, "Don't be a chump, Annie. Look out for number one." He also loved phrases like "number one. *I'm not going to be Heather Latterimer's chump, that's for sure.*

"Good luck on being a mommy," she imagined Mariel saying. Annie had done these quiet fantasy conversations many times since Mariel's death. "Mrs. Latterimer is more than willing to give you her little problem."

"I'm *not* a dummy, I'm aware."

"Are you? And when the child dies – and she *will* die – what then? How will you feel?"

"– Like shit."

A large Black lacquered divider with paintings of oriental women in pink and silver kimonos partitioned off the bed area from the rest of the narrow one room apartment. Moonlight came in through the half open window and made shadows from the angles and corners. Late night traffic could be heard on the street below her. Madrid was the same as any big city, people were always doing something.

"Why put yourself through that?" Annie could feel Mariel's breath on the edge of her left ear, the words a whisper. Even Mariel imagined became too real. *All of it phony,* Annie always reminding herself. How difficult: to give up talks with the person who'd been the center of your world.

Then Mariel said, "I don't know if I could do what you did for me. If the tables were turned. Being there, day after day, watching my bones rot. That's asking too much from people."

"I'm not people. And I did it without you asking."

"I know, my dear Beatle Paul. But why do it again?"

"She's a *kid*. She's going to need someone."

"That's what mothers are for."

"– Not that mother. You can't walk away from a child, your own child." Annie tried to picture Mariel sitting at the foot of the bed, a healthy Mariel with her dark hair and lovely big eyes. She'd been the pretty one, the smart one, the person who'd cared for Annie like nobody else. "You can't give up on them, no matter how scared you are.

I can't, anyway."

"It isn't just taking care of a sick child, is it?" Mariel said. Annie imagined the voice as soft and on the edge of pity. *Poor fool me, that's what I hear in your words.* Then Mariel said, "You think you can protect that child from the Taylor Banes of the world? From the woman you saw this afternoon?"

"Her mother won't do it."

"– Oh, Annie." Pity again, unmistakable this time.

"Don't 'Oh Annie' me, okay?"

Annie had shaved her own head. Solidarity, Annie called it. Mariel had smiled and said, "– My sentimental Annie."

"You and I, we were never Wonder Woman types. But didn't you love her costume and that invisible plane?" The laughter was breathy, distant. "You can't even protect yourself, let alone you and a sick kid? Don't you know that?"

"– No. I know nothing of the sort."

When I think about protecting myself, I am fifteen and tied down in a dark place, cold metal, water dripping. I see the steam of my breath. I see the Grays with their large dark eyes as I spread my legs. The Grays are not happy or angry or sad, I'm not sure how they feel.

But I hear them breathing.

"The cops are no help," I tell her. I say it quietly so I won't wake Beth Lee. "A guy would have to shoot and miss before they'd do anything. Hopefully the guy would miss."

ANNIE HAD STARTED reading the Grendel diary again, the placed she'd left off before her thinking rant on Mariel. *A world that isn't mine sounds very good about now.* But wasn't this woman in the diary the same woman she'd seen out her window at the Prado studio and again at the Jardin Botanico? *Well don't say that out loud.* People live and die, that law doesn't happen *some* of the time – it *always* happens. *There is such a thing as too much imagination.*

I was drawn to Liesbet, no mistake about that. Later I'd learned that she had watched me without my knowledge and found me appealing.

"I liked the paint in your hair." she'd said this the first night we made love and slept side by side.

"Just paint in the hair?"

Who loves for such a reason? I wasn't complaining. Bewildered, perhaps, but I am not a complainer. Women neither see me as pleasant or repellent. I am invisible to them. This has been my fate, what memory has shown me. But in all fairness, I am not the sort that likes to make myself known. My mother - please rest her loving and good soul - would say, "You kept too much to the shadows. Let people see what you have to offer, Luc." I know that is true but I prefer not being seen - the simple life, the uncomplicated life, I am comfortable there. An artist has a limited time on the earth like everyone else. There are very few hours to do what must be done. Art is only part time for people who have no talent for it. Yet these are excuses: I am invisible, not stupid. I know I am weak, I know I am a coward. If I were a handsome man, women would seek me out and I could dodge the blows to my pride. My life would be easier as a handsome man, filled with success. I could pick and choose and never fail. I confess to that daydream. I am guilty, take me away, lock me up, put me in the stockades. What man doesn't find relief in that? Too bad I am the person I am, invisible to even the most homely of women. Any reason for someone to love me is a good enough reason. The lame, the dim-witted, the deformed, even the blind - especially the blind, may the lord love and protect them - it does not matter.

So to have Liesbet wrapped in her white cape, plump, luscious, hungry Liesbet - what good fortune. That is what I say, what good fortune! Though I must confess, I avoid her eyes. Her eyes look too deep into me. Her eyes hurt my skin. They burn the inside of my chest, or maybe this is only the passion I feel. It does not matter that I am loved for the paint flecked in my hair. Better than not being loved, I say.

I had looked after her for less than three weeks before we shared my bed. I found her in an alley behind a smokehouse at the far end of our town. She was cut and bloody, her dress and cape torn, filthy from mud, urine and shit. The women of the town had stoned her. They squatted to piss and shit on her, too. This does not surprise me. I can imagine the women of our town doing just that and enjoying it. They are very strong women. Their aprons surely held many stones.

What amazed was the speed of Liesbet's recovery. I have never seen a person's wounds and bruises heal so quickly. Wait, I am not being honest. On *our first night in the bed together, I saw an older scar that had not healed* well at all…

THE DIGITAL CLOCK on the nightstand read 3:12 AM. Beth Lee hadn't moved. Still asleep, the child's head and right arm rested on Annie's lap. She was snoring pretty good, too. It's surprising how loud a kid can snore. Annie kissed the top of her head. The girl had that leftover heat-of-the-day smell – a mix of dried sweat and an earthy grass scent – not altogether unpleasant. She wore a sleeveless undershirt and pink cotton shorts with a picture of Barbie on the one and only pocket in the back. Probably an item picked out by the wearer. *I'm going to have a talk with your mama,*

Annie thought. *I'm already a fool for you and that can only get worse. All I need is to have another person I love die on me.* Immediately Annie pictured Heather Latterimer trying to palm her daughter off.

Shit. I'm another Heather. You can't escape from it. There is always that tension, and Annie knew it, that tension between the pleasure of loving somebody and fear of being destroyed by them.

"Oh poor Beatle Paul. What will you do?" Mariel again: she never talked this much when she was alive.

3:15 AM now. Nobody should have to mess with the imagination of a tired mind. Annie Silva knew that even at this ungodly hour...*especially* at this ungodly hour. There was no way you could win. Your imagination was more than happy to parade out every bad, pain in the ass fantasy your secret stash possessed. Remember this one? How about that one?

Then Mariel whispered, "You're doing a good thing, Annie. You're right. Trust yourself and don't run from her. She does needs you. And she's a very lucky little girl. I know, I was a lucky girl, too."

"– Shit." Annie could feel the heat rising behind her eyes. "I can't believe I'm making myself cry. God I *am* tired."

"We had some good cries, didn't we?"

"I don't want to think about it."

"You're always thinking about it." Mariel's voice was distant, fading off.

"Yeah, yeah. I know."

ONE MORE PAGE, Annie Thought. She'd placed Beth Lee next to her, tucking the pale blue sheet about the child's shoulders. The lamp on the nightstand gave the darkness a single bright smug. *There must be more than one woman who has owned a white cape. "Synchronicity," is what people call it – where two unlikely related events appear related.* Annie hoped that was true. Anything else went way beyond what she considered ... well ... reasonable. *Someone who lived forever; at the very least, a damn long time. Or not a person at all – then what, what would THAT be?* She lay on her left side, facing the light of the lamp, her hand holding the Grendel diary open and in place.

"Why are you doing this?" Liesbet said. She had awoken in my bed as I was washing and applying ointment to her wounds, what town's women and the constant blows of their stones had done to her. I'd removed the soiled cape and dress to clean these cuts and to wash off the stench, the shit and the piss. Liesbet did not seem disturbed by our situation. She was more curious than embarrassed or ashamed. No, perhaps not curious - 'Suspicious,' that would be a truer word. "Fixing my wounds, washing me - did you just want to undress me?"

"I've undressed better," I said. I hadn't, of course.

"Why help me at all?"

"I knew you," I told her. "The day you came to my house and wanted a job posing for me. You said there was no work, that no one would hire you. Why do they hate you, these women?"

"I said you had interesting hair, too." She looked at me, as if trying to figure out what sort of odd man was tending to her. "I'm surprised you don't remember that. Most men remember compliments. I liked the bits of paint, you have such a colorful mess of hair."

"Then I had said, "To be honest, I saw you on the ground near the smokehouse and took pity."

"I don't need your pity."

"Oh yes you do. Today you do."

Meeting on the Steps to Hades

When she turned over for me to apply ointment on her back, I saw an old burn patch above her shoulder blades the size of a big fist. Her skin there was smooth and pink and folded at angles, an unsettling clump of flesh. I felt repulsed by it, even nauseated. Wasn't much to the patch, really. Why I reacted that way, I'll never understand. I recall thinking how the patch resembled the profile of a goat.

10

Parked in the Mini Cooper
Carmel, California

Boring Eddy discusses business with Martinez

"TELL ME AGAIN what you did?'

"I did what you said."

Eddy released an audible breath. "Tell me again."

"I shot her twice in the head." Deputy Martinez said. "Like the instructions told me to do."

He was getting a little anxious now. Eddy liked that. Eddy also liked a good head shot.

They were sitting in a rented black and gold Mini Cooper – twelve, twelve-thirty at night, or in the morning, depending on how you looked at it. But a nice cool night, the breeze damp from the bay. The car was parked off road, the exact spot where Martinez shot Winifred Bane.

"A good beginning," Eddy said. "Then what?"

"I put her in the bag."

"Zipped it up?"

"No, left it open."

"I hope we're being amusing," Boring Eddy said.

"You got no sense of humor. Has anybody told you that? Like zero." The deputy sat on the driver's side, hands on the steering wheel. He was a short man with big overdeveloped arms. The fingertips of his right hand tapped the rim of the wheel. Eddy liked that, too – the tapping shit. Was there anything more pathetic than big arms on a nervous man? "You got to lighten up," Martinez said. "Be a person. Develop humor. People like a man with a sense of, you know, humor."

"– One of my many faults."

"– Faults? Who's saying that? Jesus, Eddy. Am I saying it's a fault? Is that how you're perceiving this – a criticism?"

The windows were rolled down in the Mini Cooper. The late morning air was warm and damp. A breeze from the ocean below them drifted through the car. The deputy's khaki shirt had the spreading darkness of sweat under his arms.

"A man can always improve himself," Boring Eddy said. Today Eddy was dressed in yellow silk Tommy Bahama with an embroidered martini glass on the back.

Vintage Hawaiian. He also had on his gray pleaded linens and his two-tone black and whites. The man was hummin'. "You should know that about yours truly, I am never above learning. I mean I hear what people call me – that boring Eddy shit. Believe me, I hear. So I said to myself, 'Eddy, you got to change your style.' A person can always learn. I'm not a what-you-call-it."

"– Asshole?"

"I was going for know-it-all."

"– Exactly. I've never considered you the know-it-all type."

"Maybe you could teach me a few jokes."

"Oh. Hey. Eddy. I'm there for you, man."

"You're the go-to guy, huh?"

"– A hundred percent go-to." The fingertips of both Martinez's hands were tapping the steering wheel like crazy now. The Rockettes of fuckin fingers, that's how Eddy saw it. Then Martinez said, "You and me, Eddy. We'd be great together, honest to God."

"You mean like, what, a date?"

"Hey, that's not me, okay?" A little too defensive.

"You got a prejudice streak, Alec. Anybody ever tell you that?"

"No, no, I'm not against shit. Nothing's wrong with it."

"Good, you shouldn't pass judgment."

"I agree a hundred percent, Eddy, believe me. Live and let live. 'Keep your nose out of other people's bedrooms,' my Motto, exactly." Martinez was sitting in the parked Mini but he kept staring ahead and moving and tapping the steering wheel like he was in a race that no one else could see. "I'm just sayin' it's not my *lifestyle*, that's all. You know, the gay thing. Ass pumping, I don't know what you call it. 'Packing the fudge,' I heard a guy say that one once – 'fudge packing.' Pretty funny, huh, if you think about it? But somebody's thing in your ass, who can do that? I don't even like my doctor sticking his finger up there. My doc sticks his finger up there and I'm thinking, 'Does he *like* doing that?' Swear to God, Eddy. I'm thinking, 'Does he think *I* like him doing that?' I always want to ask, is there another way? Like an x-ray? Or a nurse?"

"I got a couple of faggot friends," Eddy said.

"Okay, all right." Martinez started to tap the steering wheel louder and with no particular rhythm. "Good, very *good*. That's like your liberal nature, or what-have-you. Excellent."

"Occasionally I let 'em blow me. It quiets them down, you know. Keep their lips in shape, like a trumpet player."

"Eddy, I didn't mean you were –"

"Hey. I'm kidding. See I got humor."

"– *Ah*, okay, right. I get it, *very* funny. Wow."

If I were truly angry, I'd shoot you."

"Look, Eddy. I didn't mean –"

"It's a joke. Relax."

AFTER ALEC MARTINEZ had shot Winifred Bane twice in the forehead, he got out of the limo and sat next to her in the backseat and lighted a cigarette, watching the stars and the night sky through the open sunroof. Like they'd just had sex or something. The deputy stared at her for a minute, maybe two, nothing precise timewise. He blew a couple of smoke rings. He tidied up the seat with rages and a liquid leather cleaner. Then Martinez squeezed her right tit. It was like squeezing the side of a building.

"I knew it, Goddamnit."

He'd briefly thought about having sex with her. It wasn't like she'd been dead a long time, but the deceased let go of their bladder and bowel functions right away and her body smelled of urine and feces. Martinez had known he wanted to fuck Winifred Bane from the moment he saw her waiting outside his office. The odor wasn't that big of a game changer. Maybe could still fuck her, maybe feel the inside of her thigh, maybe beat-off. Something.

There ought to be a perk.

"I tell you my plan, babe," Deputy Martinez whispered to the dead Mrs. Freddie Bane. He was watching the two holes in her forehead trickle blood over her eyes like a stigmata. "This ten grand your shit-for-brains husband gave me to kill you is just the beginning, sweetheart. A hint of riches to come, if you get the drift. He's gonna retire me to the city of my choice – I'm thinking Paris. You like Paris, baby? I bet you do – or did. "*Aimez-moi, fille morte*," Martinez had said to dead Freddie. "Didn't know I spoke the language, did you, baby. Thought I was some inbred little toad who saw his badge as the highlight of his life. Too bad you never got to know me. And vice versa, lots of vice versa."

Martinez had instructions – a what-to-do list – and nobody was going to say he hadn't follow that list. *We're talkin' to the T, brother. One, I put her in the green plastic body bag. Two, I take her to this out of the way dock in the middle of the goddamn night.*

Three, the lady and I go out on the boat. Four, I wrap the chains with the weights around the bag.

Martinez had done it all. After he'd finished each instruction, he made a check mark by it on the list. The toughest part was easing the bag off the side of the boat and watching the late but still semi-hot Winifred Bane sink into Carmel Bay.

What a fucking waste.

Tonight when Alec Martinez was leaving home to meet Eddy, the real shit hit the real fan. The Mrs. sat down in *his* baby blue recliner, arms folded in front of her, wearing the pink terry cloth robe and matching slippers he'd gotten her for her thirty-eighth birthday last May.

"This is the second night in a row. You know what *time* it is?" She was in his face without leaving the recliner. Monique Lynn Martinez had short, tightly curled blond hair and a skinny body. She was also a foot and a half taller than her husband. Monique had been huffing a Pall Mall, blowing out thin angry streams of smoke.

"Hey go to bed." He did *not* want to deal with Monique.

"That's it? That's all you got?"

"I have business. Go to bed."

"Does this business involve your dick?"

"Go to *bed*, Monique." As Deputy Martinez opened the front door, he turned to look at her. "And get the fuck out of my recliner? Who gave you permission? The recliner is off limits – eternally."

"You see this?" Monique parted her pink birthday robe. "This shit will be *eternally* off limits unless I get a conversation."

Okay, point taken.

"This has to do with money," Martinez said about his meeting. "I don't know what's happened to you, Monique. What's happen to trust, baby."

"Don't do that 'baby' business."

"A *lot* of money – are you listening?" Martinez tried to give her his most sincere voice. Funny thing: the 'lot of money' part was legitimate. This Taylor Bane guy, a man running for the senate – wanting his traitor wife gone – it was the life changing job he'd wished for but could never grab. The possibilities for more money than the Lord had been revealed to him as Winifred Bane and her body bag slip into the everlasting folds of Carmel bay. "I mean it'd be the first time – you actually listening and all – but try to get out of your attitude long enough to hear me."

"This better be good – seriously good."

"You and me – Mr. and Mrs. Alec Martinez – living in *Europe* – it's that sort of money. How's that, is that seriously good?" As Martinez talked about this, he started to get excited himself. *Shit, I can do this, man. Sitting outside La Fontaine Saint-Michel, sipping wine, wearing my shades and watching the women – the FRENCH women.* "It's Europe money," he said to his wife. "It's Paris, France money – *that* sort of money. How many times have you told me how you wanted to go to Paris? About a gazillion? Now get out of my recliner."

Fine. Monique knew when to go to bed.

"I'M PRESUMING YOU got my ten?" Martinez said, meaning the ten thousand for killing Taylor Bane's wife. Martinez and Eddy were still parked on the side of the coastline road in the rented black and gold Mini Cooper, the same spot Martinez shot the Bane woman, two nicely placed ones in the forehead. Though to be fair, if you shoot someone two feet away, you can place anything nicely. "I didn't do this shit for free," Martinez said, a big enough man to admit the obvious. "I want my ten."

"That's why we're here, my man."

"I'm not your man."

"It's an expression," Eddy said.

"I know what it is. But it's an insult to my people."

"Excuse me?" Eddy couldn't believe this moron. "Where do you get the 'my people' stuff? 'My people' – who are you now? Chávez? What the fuck do your people have to do with *our* business?"

"I'm Mexican. I'm a representative."

"What – like in politics?" Eddy absently touches a palm to his brown slicked back hair. He can feel himself getting annoyed. He doesn't like getting annoyed. He particularly doesn't like getting annoyed with people who shouldn't be annoying him.

"I tell you what, Deputy, after we conclude our transaction today, why don't you take a little trot back to the old country."

"That's not what you want me to do."

"Oh really? What do I want you to do?"

"Investigate the murder," Martinez said and grinned. Eddy thought the guy had nice teeth, very even, very white.

Eddy was looking forward to killing the Mexican. Taylor Bane had suggested he "put a bow on it." The Mexican kills the wife. Eddy kills the Mexican. It sounded good, it had a symmetry – the bow of bows, so-to-speak. But Taylor could be too impulsive. Two deaths so close together in a small town, not the smartest play. People aren't stupid. What Eddy needed was an investigation guaranteed to go nowhere.

Okay, my friend. You're luckier than you know.

"Maybe I should start calling you 'Mr. Representative.' Bet you'd like that."

Eddy tried to match Martinez grin for grin, keeping it light, keeping it buddy-buddy.

"But 'representative' of what, that's the question. Your interest? Mine? Have you noticed how all the great question are about what and who?"

"What, who, I don't give a shit. The Mexican is good enough to cut your grass and pick your produce, but we can't date your daughters."

"You're right, Martinez. You can't date my daughter." I'm not married. And I don't have a daughter. But if I *was* married and if I *had* a daughter, I'd tell you to cut my grass and leave my daughter alone."

Eddy thought this was pretty funny. Martinez didn't laugh, the putz. Try to be charming and what does it get you? Nothing but a bad look. Everybody has a sense of humor except when it comes to them, then the world turns, then things aren't funny.

"How about my money," Martinez said.

Eddy reached into the glove compartment – the Glove Box Organizer – of the Mini Cooper and handed a fat white envelope to the deputy. Immediately the asshole opens it and starts fingering the money like he can count.

"– Not enough," Martinez said; doesn't look up from the open envelope.

"I counted it twice, ten thousand. "You mean it's short?"

"I mean it's fifty thousand."

"The contract was ten."

"I think it's fifty."

Eddy looked at the Mexican. *Forget Hugo Chávez. This is Poncho fuckin Villa.*

The night air from the bay was getting to him. Eddy felt a line of sweat go down the back of his shirt. He hated sweating. Maybe not as much as he hated this Mexican but he hated it.

"So what are you telling me?" Eddy said.

"I'm telling you fifty."

"What, ten isn't good enough? Now you want fifty?" Eddy shook his head as if he was reluctantly admiring the asshole's balls. "I'm guessing this won't be the last fifty you'll want. When will you want another?"

"I'll want it when I want it."

"Ah, okay, this is what I thought. So conceivably we're going to be friends for a long time. Is that what you're telling me?"

"– Conceivably. It's a good word."

Eddy took a small Beretta Px4 Storm from the holster under his suitcoat and shot Martinez once in his right eye. Blood and bits of brain and skull stuck to the tan leather interior and the windshield. He thought the same thing the Mexican had thought when he'd killed Mrs. Bane.

Everybody's a good shot close up.

11

Calle Ruiz de Alarcon
Madrid

The disappearance

THE WOMAN FROM the park stood on the balcony near the closed double glass doors. Beth Lee could see her in the moonlight. She was wearing her pretty white cape. Sometimes the woman looked exactly like Beth's mother – who preferred being called "Heather" – tall, slender, blond stringy hair – then the woman would shift back again and become a shorter person with much heavier legs. She kept going back and forth like one of those slow blinking neon signs, first this followed by that, but Beth didn't feel afraid. No matter the woman's appearance at the moment, she always had a nice smile. The girl thought it was a dream or maybe a trick. People didn't change like that.

"I can't play now," Beth whispered.

The woman waved a small piece of paper in one hand and she signaled the girl to come to the balcony – never without a smile, though. Moonlight surrounded the woman and gave her hair and shoulders a silver look.

"– Go home," the girl said, another whisper.

Beth Lee drew the bed sheet over her head and shut her eyes. Heather once told her that a bad dream can go away if you hide from it and shut your eyes real, real tight.

For most dreams this advice worked very well. When Beth's mother was in the mood, she knew what to do and how to help. But this time the advice wasn't working. Beth glanced over the sheet and saw the woman kneeling beside the bed. There were also shadows near the bed, some shaped like people, some like large birds. Immediately the shadows blended into a darkness that hid most of the woman except a sliver of her face.

She looked as if she was peering through the slit of two curtains.

"You're not my mother," Beth said.

"No, I'm Liesbet."

"– You're a dream."

"Well aren't we the brightest little thing," Liesbet said, not leaving the shadows. Moonlight came in through the still closed glass doors and showed the hem of her white cape. "I'd say I'm almost *in* a dream. But better, oh much better."

"I didn't invite you here." The girl had folded her arms, her chin jutting out, looking very defiant.

"I go where I'm needed."

Beth felt a cool dry hand begin to stroke her forehead. Her whole body shivered to its touch. The muscles in her shoulders, tummy and legs turned warm and loose, every part of her sinking into the deep softness of the bed.

"You'd like a lot more of this," Liesbet said, meaning her touch.

"– Yes."

"It takes the pain away."

"– Yes."

"And the pain is everywhere, isn't it? Most every day."

Beth nodded, her eyes closed.

"You feel the pain between your toes and fingers," Liesbet whispered. "– In your very bones – even behind your eyes – and you want so very much to get away from it but you can't. No one has helped you, not the doctor, not your mama."

"– Mamma's afraid."

"Our mamas need to be strong for us."

"She says, 'Beth Lee, Mommy's nerves can't take it.' Mama loves me too much, that's what she says."

"Maybe you need a momma who can take it." The palm of Liesbet's hand rested on the child's gaunt cheek. "Somebody tough."

The girl was propped up on the bed, her back against a feather pillow and the dark wood of the headboard. Annie slept next to her, a sleep so silent and peaceful that once during the night Beth had leaned in to hear her breathe.

"Annie's tough," Beth said, defending her new friend.

"But can she take the pain away?" Liesbet lifted Beth up and pressed the child to her, a strong-arm cradling Beth's back.

"Is this a dream or real?"

"– Something in between." The woman kissed her warm forehead. "How do you feel now?"

"– I feel ... good."

"See. This is what I can do for you." Liesbet placed the note she'd been holding on the pillow.

"What does that say?" Beth wanted to know.

"It says you and I are visiting."

"– In the in-between place?"

"Right, *yes*. That's it, exactly, the in-between place. Such a smart girl."

WHEN ANNIE WOKE in the morning, Beth Lee was gone. On her pillow lay a small leaf of yellow parchment with two well printed sentences in black ink. An ancient look, Annie thought, not unlike the handwriting of Luc Grendel's diary.

You tell no one. Wait for me to contact you.

A second or two had to pass before she could shake off her sleepy indifference.

The morning already felt sticky and hot. Sunlight reflected off rumpled white sheets, the hard wood floors. Annie had to hold her hand to her brow to keep the light from hurting her eyes. Madrid was the brightest city she'd ever been to. No one escaped the Madrid sun. The light seemed to show itself everywhere at once. In the morning and afternoon you couldn't find your own shadow.

–*Where's the kid?* Thinking it, her mind still bloated with sleep. She looked at the bit of parchment again. *Tell no one what?* Then her hand touched the vacant pillow.

She lifted the sheet and peeked. *Wasn't the child skinny enough to hide between the folds?* That was when it all became clear.

You tell no one. Wait for me to contact you.

– Shit, shit ...

What have I done?

Annie leaned her head down and looked under the bed. Nothing. *God of course nothing, what kid hides under the bed anymore? Every TV show has a dead body under there. Kids aren't stupid.* Annie tried sliding out of the bed but about halfway through it she caught her right foot in the sheet and fell to the floor. She shut her eyes, took a breath and glanced up at the rotating ceiling fan.

"– Beth."

Maybe her voice was too quiet.

"– Beth!"

No answer.

That was when all things came into focus.

– Kidnaped.

As the word came to mind, it brought panic.

Good morning, a female voice said in her head – something imagined, something to take the edge off and calm Annie down – one of those pleasant voice-overs on a TV travelogue: *Welcome to another day in beautiful Madrid. Enjoy fine dining at our many restaurants. Visit our museums and art galleries. See bullfights in exciting Vista Alegre and Las Ventas. Young Americans who squeal and faint are particularly encouraged.*

Oh. And the little girl under your care?

Kidnaped.

"Beth?" Then louder, "– Beth? Hel-*lo*?" Annie stood and pressed her fingertips into the sore spot at the small of her back. She began her search. *Please be here, please let this be a cruel kid game.* "You in the bathroom, sweetie?" Annie walked from the partitioned sleeping area to the narrow main room. Skylights and windows let the sun in, the apartment filled with intense morning light. "Hey, Beth – if you *are* playing a game? – I'm new to the mommy business, okay? Don't scare me."

– Shit, shit ...

That was all that came to mind.

The phone rang – once, twice. Annie guessed it was Mrs. Heather Latterimer, the I-am-way-Too-Anxious-To-Be-With-My-Daughter-But-If-You-Lose

Her-I-will-Feel Enough-Guilt-To-Come-Down-On-You-Like-The-Apocalypse...mommy.

"Good morning," Heather said.

"Can I call you back?"

"How's my little angel?"

"Great, great," Annie said. "– Really."

IN THE VERY early morning, Liesbet had gone to her fourth-floor apartment in the Plaza Mayor, part of what people called Old Madrid. She'd walked into the bedroom with Beth Lee asleep in her arms. The cape hid much of the child. An open balcony let warm damn air to the room, and dawn threaded the sky pink. The woman lay Beth on the double bed and adjusted the cotton sheet about her thin shoulders.

"– Not to have pain," Liesbet said as she leaned down and kissed the child's forehead. "While you're with me, I can give you that."

Beth looked even more fragile and small in the bed. The mahogany head and foot boards and the four thick posts surrounded her like a dark unclimbable wall.

Tricks were not Liesbet Grendel favorite way of doing business. She liked to go by whatever rules governed people and place. Don't disturb the landscape – your house, your rules, that sort of thing. You don't have to keep to the shadows but you don't walk naked in the streets.

The last person Liesbet had helped to sleep was her husband Luc – not so much helped to sleep as let him join her, let him go to the in-between place. That was what she'd called it with him, too. "Come to the In Between with me, dear Luc. Let me show you a place that isn't a dream but isn't what you'd call 'real,' either. Most artists find it all very curious." Liesbet thought Luc would find it curious, too. She'd taken him to visit her town, to meet her friends, to see her rules.

"Where am I?" he had said, so horrified, so ... paralyzed.

"– Breathe," she told him.

"– I-I can't."

"– *Breathe!*" Liesbet pressed her hands to his chest and his back and pushed and pulled him like an accordion until he gasped and started breathing on his own. "There are strange rules everywhere. Don't you agree, husband? You must. Think of being here as learning about a foreign country – isn't that what it is? – no different than, say, England or Germany? Different ways of acting, yes, of course. But similarities, too.

Don't we all suffer, find joy between the cracks? In the end, aren't we all foreigners somewhere?"

"What is this place?"

"My home, Luc."

They had walked through a relentless smoky dimness, passed many gold doors and down the spiral stairway of many gray cobblestone steps. He had noticed stars and tiny suns and half-moons cut deep into each door. There were scratches on the doors he didn't understand. A language, perhaps. Luc was also sure the stairs had patches of blood on them. The blood had dried about the stones and in the uneven grooves between the stones.

"What has happened here?" Luc knelt and touched the blood, or whatever it was, then sniffed his fingertips. The odor reminded him of rotting wood. "These stains are everywhere, up and down the steps."

"Old battles," Liesbet said. "I don't know."

"How can you not know?" That seemed incomprehensible to him.

"I was born into this. Without explanation."

"What does that mean 'without explanation?' Certainly the locals talk; certainly stories are told." Then he said, "You had parents. You had people who ... instructed you.

Teachers. People who answered your question. Or some questions."

"How can you be so sure?"

"If you don't know about the stairs, tell me about these gold doors – there are so many. Or do you also *not* know about that?"

"They're residences – homes –very coveted, very lovely. I *do* know that, I live in one." Liesbet heard the pride in her voice and smiled. "Those of us who've been given homes along this walkway spend much of our time in –" she hesitated, thinking of what he might or might not understand "– the foreign service. Does that make sense? We go to different places to do our work. These homes are given to us like a king would bestow a title."

"– A title?" He looked utterly confused.

"Yes, like a ... knight."

"So you're a – what? – a soldier?"

"No, no. I just don't know how else to explain it."

Liesbet knew Luc had wanted to ask her about that, too – she imagined the man saying, 'What do you mean by 'service?' What sort of service?' – but he'd paused at the last step of the walkway to look out at the village and the mountains beyond the village and the smoky tracks in an orange tinted sky.

"– My God."

"Lovely, isn't it?"

"I wouldn't call it that. No, 'lovely' isn't the word."

"I KNEW IT," Heather Latterimer had said. She'd said this when Annie told her over the phone how great everything was going with Beth Lee.

First lie of the morning. I open my eyes and immediately start lying. Wonderful.

I don't even think about whether it's a lie or not. Whatever people want, whatever the situations calls for, whatever will keep the peace.

"See, people don't think I know my child but I know," Heather said. "Believe me, I *get* my daughter. You're what my baby needs, Annie. What the doctor ordered.

God I shouldn't joke. Let me speak to her. Mommy wants to say good morning."

"– Still asleep," Annie whispered, looking at the empty bed. *Jesus. Liar, liar pants fire.*

"*Oooo*, okay, okay," Heather now whispering, too.

"She's get tired easily."

"Oh you don't have to tell me. Poor thing."

"– Uh, listen," Annie said and took an audible breath. A thought had occurred to her – more an on-the-fly plan. "Now that I have you on the phone." *God, be casual. Stay calm, just a couple of folks concerned about the little girl they love.* "Why don't I take Beth for a couple of days. You know, give you a break. Not that you need one, I'm not saying that. You're one remarkable mom. I know I couldn't handle what you're going through."

"You'd do that?" Heather sounded bewildered, stunned.

"I'm what the doctor ordered, right? Am I right, or what?"

"Oh abso*lute*ly right. A hundred percent."

"Okay. *Okay* then." Annie wasn't sure how long she could stretch out Mrs. Latterimer's vacation from the daughter she both loved and feared, but Annie figured three days, four tops. "I'm glad just I can do something for you, Heather. May I call you Heather?"

"Call me what you want," the woman said, almost giddy.

Oh don't tempt me. "Well some people prefer, you know, formality. I don't want to offend."

"Hey, be comfortable, I say. I'm so happy my child has found a friend. You know, sometimes friends are better at this than the parents."

Annie knew better than to tell Heather Latterimer the truth.

She could imagine it, though, what she'd say to Beth's mother. *We DO get along fine,* Annie would say, *and I love her to death. I honestly do, I can tell you that and know in my heart it's true. I mean who wouldn't love this kid? She's sweet and funny, and she loves you back like there is no tomorrow. I mean Beth doesn't just hug you she grabs your neck and won't let go. Serious hugs. Which is fine with me, by the way. But now I have terrible news, the worst news ever. When I woke up this morning, there was no one in the bed but me. Beth Lee is gone, Heather – may I call you heather? – simply and completely GONE. I don't know where the fuck she is. I'm talking not a clue, okay, not one. And this isn't being said to scare you, Heather. We both know you're scared enough. Psycho ward material, if you ask me. Heavy medication. Around the clock supervision. It's a wonder you can stay inside your skin. I just want time to make it right, time to get her back.*

You tell no one. Wait for me to contact you.

If I don't get a 'contact' in the next hour, I'm looking for you.

"Are you all right, dear?" Mrs. Latterimer said.

"– What?"

"Are you all right?"

No, I'm not all right. No, ma'am. I need to get off this phone. The angry part of Annie surprised her. *I need to stop hearing your creepy, grateful voice. I'm not here to get you off the hook with your daughter. That wish is only in your head. How 'bout I tell you what I think is really going on and see how all right you'll be? How 'bout that?*

"Oh God, yes. Fine," Annie said.

"Tell Beth to call mommy's cell."

"– Uh-huh."

THE CHILD WOULD sleep until Liesbet Grendel woke her, and that should be soon. Good bargaining required something to bargain with, a little leverage. You give me this and I'll give you that. Liesbet closed the bedroom door and locked it. Here in her fourth-floor apartment of the Plaza Mayor, no one would disturb them. She liked this girl, this *very* sick girl. The woman hadn't missed raising a child for a long time until she held Beth Lee's small body against her chest. That left her feeling alone and regretful. *But maybe I'm not the mothering sort*, Liesbet thought. *I kill as easily as I comfort. That always bothered me – what if I'd hurt her. My child, my own child. I can forgive myself almost anything but that.*

She could smell the bacon and the pork, the fresh bread. What always began the morning when it was still dark were the heady cooking and baking smells coming from the restaurants. Once the large 17th century square below her had been used to execute heretics. Muslims and Jews, mostly. Now shopkeepers, bars and eateries competed for the tourist trade. Liesbet knew they'd start the executions again if meant getting more tourists.

Perhaps she'd have a *carajillo* and sit on the balcony and sip her drink and watch the sunrise and the workers preparing for the day – hosing down and sweeping the shop fronts, the unfurling of colorful tablecloths for outside the cafes, blue, red, white, green. This was always a good hour to think about what needed to be done.

Liesbet's dream had allowed Luc Grendel to enter her world. As she got closer to reclaiming his painting and the diary – what was always called "the betrayals" – she remembered more detail about his encounter with the perpetual night and glow of her town. How astonished the painter had looked. There were no changing seasons, Liesbet explained. The day did not become brighter or grow into evening or *become* something, rainy, windy, cold, warm, etcetera. "On the positive side," she had said – an attempt to relax him – "one never needed to dress for the weather." She even laughed a bit, hoping he would join her but he didn't. Or couldn't. There was an orange tint to the night and it became more red than orange along the mountain ridge. Traces of smoke or fog stayed nestled about the town. The fog had allowed the hand to touch his face. Liesbet could understand Luc's terror as the thing emerged – hair black and fine, its extraordinary long fingers. And the silver nails, he never forgot the nails.

12

Poolside at the Bane Home
Monterey, California

On what to do with the Grendel woman

"SO YOU TRUST HER, or what?"

"How long you know me?" Taylor Bane said. He was trying to figure his rummy hand. He had shit for cards.

"– Too long."

"Then you know I don't trust my own mother. Who's basically a total saint. Ask anybody – give you her last dime. What can I say? It's a glitch in my character." Bane had on a fashionable wrinkled white linen suit, a black V-neck T, and sandals. "If I'd say, 'Hey, Ma, I killed a guy last night.' She'd tell me it's a what-you-call-it, a *phase*, and not to worry."

The would-be senator was having this nowhere conversation with Boring Eddy.

They were drinking Tom Collins and playing rummy under the white and red umbrella next to Taylor's heart-shaped pool – the heart shape being a Winifred Bane idea, the recently missing and still undiscovered wife. Taylor had phoned the Monterey County Sheriff's Department after a respectable twenty-four hours. He also made sure to sound like a very worried husband.

"When do you turn over again? Fifteen minutes, twenty? I can never remember."

Bailey Sutton lay in the sunlight on a matching red and white chaise near his two friends.

The man's three hundred and six-two pounds of coconut buttered flesh had already gone bright pink. "Is it a specific time, or when you feel like it? What is it?"

"Just turn the fuck over," Eddy said.

"We'll kill her, too," Taylor said to Eddy.

"– the Grendel woman?"

"Loose ends are never good."

VERY LOOSE ENDS. "Were you going through my things?" Taylor said this to Freddie two days before their 19th anniversary.

"I don't touch your things."

"Yeah, you do."

They were in the bathroom. She was in the middle of eyeliner, a white towel wrapped about her tall, ample body; another towel wrapped turban style about her wet hair. He leaned against the doorway, watching her. The 19th was another endurance year. As in, *God, has it only been 19 years?* Nothing special. You got topaz jewelry, maybe something bronze, it was an off year. Nothing like the twentieth, on the twentieth you got China. Mrs. Bane thought a person ought to get metal for the 20th. Like the silver star.

"I get accused of everything," she said.

"That's because you're always where you shouldn't be. What did I tell you about going through my things."

Freddie continued with the eyeliner, her hand a little shaky. "– Shit." Now she'd practically stabbed herself with the point of the pencil. "You're making me nervous. I can't discuss this now."

"You want me to make an appointment?" Taylor said.

She glanced at him. Ten in the morning and her husband was wearing a tan Saint Laurent and a mauve shirt and matching tie. The man lived to dress.

"I want you to trust me."

"You want another person," he said.

Freddie Bane tossed the eyeliner pencil into the sink, looked down at it and took a breath. "Okay, Taylor. Let's hear your issues."

"What did you see?" Implying: she was snooping through his desk drawers.

"I didn't *see* anything."

"What did you see, darling?"

"Your whatever, your To Do list."

"– Uh-oh." Taylor grinned.

"Don't give me the 'uh-oh,' okay? 'Uh-oh' – like the world's coming to an end."

She hated him when he got like this. A person could hear the joy in his voice. "That's what you do. You're an intimidator. You like doing that, intimidating people, especially the woman who loves you."

"I trust the woman who loves me. I just don't trust you."

"– Very funny. Very *droll.*"

"Hey. C'mon, Freddie. It's a joke."

She walked past her husband without looking at him. *Asshole*, she thought. *I'm tired of letting myself feel hurt by every moronic thing you say.* Taylor watched for a second or two before following her down the hall. The ceiling of the upstairs hallway was glass and let in the morning. A shadow moved down the pine floor as a single cloud drifted through the sunlight.

"Where you going, darlin'?" Taylor tried to have a playful tone.

"I have an appointment."

"What is it, therapy day?"

"It wouldn't hurt you to go, believe me."

"LET THE BIG man kill her," Eddy said, studying his cards. Taylor had just asked him if he was going to play the damn hand or paint a picture. "Grendel creeps me out."

"Excuse me? *You* kill her," Bailey said. He had on his sunglasses with the silver lenses. Nobody could see what his eyes were doing, Taylor hated that. This was why Bailey wore them. "I'm a lover, not a fighter."

"– Right handed or left?" Eddy said. He glanced over at Taylor to see if his boss got the joke. The boss had no expression. Taylor was losing at gin rummy and he didn't like to lose at anything. Eddy looked down at his own cards again and released a breath, his shoulder slumping.

White tile surround the pool, reflecting sunlight. Bailey had an orange and navy blue striped squeeze bottle in his right hand. Every-so-often he'd spray his chest and arms with water.

"I like her," the big man said. "Charming, in her way. We got along. I thought Mrs. Grendel, you know, liked me, too. Or maybe I misread the signals – but we at least had a mutual respect. Yeah, that's it, that's what we had. The two of us, we respected each other."

"Reason enough to shoot her." Eddy muttered this to himself.

"You don't think this is serious?" This was not a good time to fuck with Taylor. There was never good time.

"Hey absolutely," Eddy said, his palms open and raised, a quick and prudent surrender. "– *Very* serious."

Then Taylor said to Bailey, "Tell us your observations."

"I'd have to think about it."

"Do that now. It's a pleasant day." Bane looked up from his cards and grinned to no one in particular, as if pleased he'd thought of a way to stop thinking about losing at rummy and start thinking about ways to torture Bailey. Maybe his wife – his very dead but still missing wife – was right. He did like torturing certain people. He liked seeing them get anxious. "We're all here, yes? All friends? You said Mrs. Grendel seemed professional."

"– *Was* professional. Not seemed."

"– What else."

Bailey turned on his side, propping himself up on an elbow. He looked at Taylor from behind the silver lenses of his sunglasses. "So all these years and you don't trust me, either? Is this about my judgment?"

"Sometimes we miss a detail," Eddy said.

"Who's talking to you?" The big man didn't need both of them on him. *Eddy the Douchebag. Always finding everything so amusing, particularly Yours Truly.* "I don't have to listen to you, *Ed*ward. Okay? How 'bout you fixing your own business. That all right? Personally, I think it's an excellent idea."

"It's just a fact," Eddy said. "We miss detail."

"Here's a detail – blow me."

Bane raised his hand. Eddy stared at the pool, the flat sunlit water. Bailey laid on his back again, closed his eyes behind silver sunglasses.

"I don't hear from her, our Mrs. Grendel," Taylor said. He squared off his rummy cards -- crappy hand to begin with – and placed them face down on the glass patio table. The umbrella shaded the cards. "She doesn't call. I pay her. I give her expenses, what she wants. Everything generous, everything above and beyond. What I get is no calls, no updates. I don't hear, 'Yeah, I've done the contract.' Or, 'No I haven't done the contract. I got a problem.' I hear nothing, the person who pays her salary is uninformed, left in the dark, so-to-speak. Our Mrs. Grendel is a silent movie." Taylor waved his hand, shaking off the subject. It's made him feel worse than the crappy rummy hand. "It's peculiar, that's all. Like I'm working for her."

Bailey used a gray and white towel to pat the sweat from his chest and large stomach before he eased himself on his side again to talk with Bane.

"Well. I recall an *attitude* from Mrs. Grendel," he said. "The woman did appear more interested in a certain painting than Annie Silva. *Meeting on the Steps to Hades,* that was the painting."

"Did she just pull that out of her ass?" Taylor felt he couldn't get a sane answer out of anybody today. "– Bring it up out of nowhere, I mean. What did you say to her *before* the painting business? Anything?"

"I told her Annie worked at the Prado in Madrid. Maybe I should have said that part first. That's where the painting is – the Prado." Bailey made a little grunting sound as he lifted himself from a reclining to a sitting position. "But Liesbet seemed to already know that."

"Liesbet? You call her that?"

"It's her name. People call her Liesbet."

"You two are what – BFFs?"

"If a client wants me to call her by her first name, I oblige."

"Take off the fucking glasses," Taylor said. "I want to see your eyes."

The big man removed his sunglasses then squinted, holding his right hand above his brow to block the sun. "The artist had her last name – some guy named Luc Grendel, a Flemish painter. A relation, she told me. Mrs. Grendel thought the job could work well with her current task."

"– Finding some painting."

"– More a family heirloom."

"So we're an appendage, second to the arts."

"Mrs. Grendel used the phrase, 'Two birds with one stone.' It seems – and I'm just guessing – but it seems she needs Annie Silva."

"Why didn't you discuss this with me?" Taylor said. He was slouched in his chair, looking at nothing in particular, the underside of the red and white umbrella. "This isn't good. This is a total nightmare. I'm paying a woman to kill somebody she *needs*? How do you think that'll turn out? Is that a winner? Or do you think we have a conflict of interests?"

"Mrs. Grendel does her job."

"Which job, that's our question." Bane took a sip of his Tom Collins, absently rattling the ice in the glass as he looked at the big man. "Remind me what the Silva woman does again?"

"She restores old paintings. A conservator."

"– At the Prado."

"Uh-huh. The restoration of the Grendel painting."

"See. That's the thing that gets me." Taylor was tapping his fingernails on the glass tabletop. Bailey always took the finger tapping as a signal – his friend's growing agitation. Rage was never far away from the finger thing. "Our Mrs. Grendel knew 'bout this from the get-go," Taylor said. "This is a planned event. Get money from us, take care of her business."

"I've talked to people. She does her job."

"– Until it doesn't," Eddy said. He crossed his tanned bare legs, ankle on knee, his sandal foot wiggling to some nervous rhythm. "A house divided and all that shit.

You got to be cautious, Taylor."

Bailey looked at Eddy and pantomimed a shush, finger to the lips. "We're talkin' here. Let the grownups finish." Before Eddy could respond, the big man had turned and was saying, "– Mrs. Grendel can't just sling that sizable painting over her shoulder and walk out of the Prado. She'll need the Silva woman's help. After that, she'll kill her."

"– What we're paying her to do," Taylor said.

THEN MRS. BANE WANTED to know about Annie Silva.

"What about her?" Taylor said, all smiles.

He'd followed her down the hallway. They were in the bedroom now. Clouds had dissipated and sunlight came through the Venetian blinds, fixing to the wood floor in long yellow bars. Freddie was picking out her clothes for the day – black and white oxfords and a thin gray striped Armani.

"This is the same Annie, isn't it?" She said, holding the Armani in front of the full-length mirror at the entrance to the walk-in closet. She wanted her conversation to sound casual, not prying. Her husband had radar for the prying thing. "– Annie and her friend Mariel, is it that Annie?"

"I'm not a memory lane type of guy."

"You're right. Too many years ago," Freddie said. "Who keeps count of all it? Adventures from an impetuous youth."

"Aren't all young people impetuous?"

"Well, you know, some more than others."

Rich boys escaping their cruel acts: Freddie knew this wasn't a good place to go.

She was sure this was *the* Annie Silva but you don't seek out a stranger with the sort of message she had to deliver unless there was no doubt who was who. You don't say, "Are you the Annie Silva my husband and his moron friends raped at a Halloween frat party?"

You have to already have the facts before you punch in the number and scare this poor woman shitless. You have to be a hundred percent sure before you tell her, "It's nothing personal, Annie. You're a roadblock, a stone to trip over. I know you were raped, hon. But it's worse now. Now you're in his way."

13

Plaza Mayor, fourth floor
Madrid

The appearance of motherly love

LIESBET GRENDEL sat in a faded red velour chair at the far corner of the bedroom, hands folded on her lap, her pose calm but vigilant. Beneath the white cape her fingers stroked a leather sheath strapped to her left forearm. The sheath contained a twelve-inch blade, very thin, very sharp. Shadow concealed this corner. Moonlight entered through the open balcony doors. The silver light lay wide and bright between Liesbet and the sleeping child.

–*What if I hurt her?* she thought.

"I trust you." Luc's voice, at least in her mind, how she remembered him. She could imagine her husband saying, "I trust you more than you trust yourself."

I kill the way animals kill. That would have been Liesbet's argument. *Without anger. Without guilt. It is a job, like a blacksmith shoeing a horse.* No, more than that. She believed killing was her calling. *I still think it. My need to kill is no different than Luc's to paint.*

What would her husband have said then? "I am glad you're pregnant. I want to be a father. I think I'd be a good one, don't you?"

"It wasn't the father that worried me," she whispered. To a moonlit bedroom. To a sleeping Beth Lee.

Liesbet had willed their child dead while it was in the womb. *Or plotted its death, that was more the way. Let me not kid myself.* She'd gone to Luc's village and did what she liked to do, stirred the men and taunted the women. More than once she walked the four or so kilometers from their cabin to the village, stepping into the cold and the wind. One night, flecks of new snow raced about her, stinging her face, her raw thick hands. She drank with the men in Cleys Pub. She laughed at their jokes and let them touch her. *It never took long for women to gather their stones.*

FR. RAFA HAD told Annie to inform the CNP, the Cuerpo Nacional de Policia about the missing girl.

"I just need time away," she'd said. In a panic? Did she sound – what? – out of control, ready to split her skin and run toady-eyed and shrieking through traffic down the Calle de Antoni Maura? *Calm down. Take a breath.* "I'm asking for a day – two, tops.

I think the person involved will contact me."

"This is a kidnapping. Kidnappings are reported."

"You've seen the mother." Annie was in her apartment and sitting on the edge of the unmade bed, still dressed in her sleeping togs, a pink undershirt and matching boxers: Truck Driver Barbie, Mariel had called it. Eight-forty-two and the sunlight was already brilliant on the white walls and the polished wood floor. "You want to screw with Mama Heather's mental state, Rafa? Peel her ass off the ceiling, excuse the language. I mean be my guest." The Prado had made Fr. Rafa their go-between – supervisor to the conservator in all things administrative. "Is that what you want?"

"What do I tell them?" the friar said.

You tell no one. Wait for me to contact you.

"Tell them I've got the flu."

"Fine. You have two days."

"– Rafa..."

Annie didn't want to quit talking but what to say? She kept the cell to her ear and shut her eyes. Fr. Rafa's breath had an even rhythm, the opposite of what she felt in her quick and frightened heart. It pushed at her neck, her ears. That startled roar, that tempo, its counterpoint so out of step with what came from him.

"Some of us have work to do," Fr. Rafa said.

"Yeah. I don't know what's wrong. I'll let you go."

"How's your faith?" he said.

"Piss poor, thanks."

"Maybe you should rethink that."

"– Shit, Rafa. I wouldn't know where to begin."

LAST NIGHT BETH Lee could not keep her eyes open – a second, maybe two, enough to peek at the moonlight on the floor and the big chair in the shadow across the room. Everything felt so heavy, her eyelids, her head, her arms and legs. The girl once had a dream where the top part of what she usually saw was painted black and she could only see her purple sneakers and the sidewalk. People would talk to her in the dream and she saw their legs from the knee down and their shoes. She thought the dream was funny and creepy but mostly creepy.

Somebody's in the big chair.

Beth Lee wanted to say to whatever was in the chair, "Are you gonna give me to the devils and the wolves?" That was what her mama said when Beth was being bad. The girl's words came out in grunty pieces. *Uh-ah-uuuh-uh.* She was always bad, if you listened to mama. The devils and the wolves waited in line for her. They argued about who was first and what parts they wanted to chew.

–Me, me, grrr, I was here!

Grrr, no.

I eat you, too. Grrr.

Everybody in line growled. They growled every moment of every day. Or that's what Beth Lee imagined: growling angry things for bad children. She'd imagined devils and wolves hiding under her bed. In the closet. In the backyard at night behind the trees. Some were heard clicking their hooves on the roof.

They could be anywhere, any moment.

"Are the wolves close now, mama? Beth's bed time question.

"– If you do bad."

"– The devils, too?"

"Oh yes. Especially the devils."

Heather Latterimer was a pretty woman -- *the* most beautiful mama, Beth thought, a mama with gold hair and many curls – but Beth couldn't look at her mother's eyes for more than a second or two. Her mama had eyes that kept moving, shaky eyes, eyes that couldn't get comfortable.

"Big children don't get scared," Beth's mother liked to say.

"– But I'm not big."

"– Big *inside.*"

Usually Mrs. Latterimer said this when her daughter complained that the bedside lamp wasn't bright enough or the door to her room wasn't opened wide enough. After ten or fifteen minutes of this, Heather Latterimer would cover her ears and say,

"Okay, okay, okay, okay," and she'd walk out of the room and shut the door. Beth had to wait a couple of minutes before getting out bed and opening the door just the right amount.

THE JARDIN BOTANICO was opposite the Museum on the Paseo del Prado. *She would be there, wouldn't she?* Annie thought. *In the park, where I first saw her? And she'd know I'd be in a panic, this isn't a stupid woman.* Annie had showered and dressed in a little over ten minutes. The morning was already warm and humid and far too bright. The traffic on the Paseo had backed up and some drivers were leaning on their horns, particularly the cabbies. *El tiempo es dinero.* Time is money. Annie jogged some and walked some. Her anxiety about the child came and went. When it came, Annie ran. She wore her jeans that were faded about the thighs and butt and frayed at the knees. She also had on a floppy brim straw hat and large sunglasses. A look earlier in the mirror with the hat and sunglasses had brought a vague Jackie Onassis aura to the image, if Jackie had been a short, semi-zoftig and Jewish.

The woman in the white cape sat on the park bench, the same wood bench Annie had first seen her from the studio window at the Prado.

Isn't that her? How many people wear a white cape in this heat. I bet the bitch doesn't even sweat.

Annie stopped a half block or so from the park. She leaned against one of the old trees that lined the Paseo and let the shade cool her. *Too early in the morning to rush all this stuff* – meaning herself. But seeing the woman had taken the life from her legs.

Annie had not forgotten her phone conversation with Mrs. Bane.

"– Liesbet Grendel." Freddie had whispered. Annie hardly heard the woman.

Maybe she'd been talking too close to the phone. "Can you hear me?"

Annie remembered telling the woman to talk louder. "– A bad connection. Or something, static on the line. Did you say Grendel?"

"Yes, *Liesbet* Grendel."

"– Like the painter?"

"The woman who's been hired...*to kill you*," Winifred Bane over pronounced each word but whispered the "to kill you" part. "Her name is *Grendel.* Okay? Can you hear that?"

"You mean like the painter?" Annie had said again.

"I don't know painters."

Yes, you didn't forget a conversation like that.

Annie was still leaning against one of the large shade trees on the Paseo, thinking about her talk with Freddie and watching the woman in the white cape who sat on the park bench. Annie would've preferred the bench to have been empty. She felt a tightness in her stomach and across her shoulders. But if the woman hadn't been there, she'd have felt anxious about that, too. Sometimes you can't win, no matter what.

Now the woman in the white cape looked at her and waved.

WHEN THE SKY was still dark, the very beginning of the morning, moonlight covered the square of the Plaza Mayor and turned the stones silver. Liesbet Grendel had left the red velour chair and stood at the open doors near the balcony. People who work at the shops and restaurants in the square begin their jobs before the sun becomes a purple streak in the darkness. A man in a chef's coat was now sitting at one of the outside cafés, playing the guitar. The chef did this each morning for a half hour, give or take – early, too – somewhere between three-thirty or four. The rhythm was always soft, complex and beautiful. Mrs. Grendel had never seen anybody step out on one the many balconies and complain. Chef and guitar came with the territory; who knew why. Perhaps he liked announcing the dawn and perhaps the residents of Plaza Mayor liked him doing it.

Beth Lee was trying to look at the woman in the white cape– head lifted slightly, trembling from the strain. Her eyes fluttered open halfway, never more than a second, perhaps two. Liesbet smiled, something quick and unnoticeable.

"You're a tough one," the woman said, kneeling beside the bed.

A few strands of blond hair showed about the sides of Beth's cap. Liesbet brushed the hair away from the girl's forehead. She was surprised how close she felt toward the child. The thought left her feeling empty and uncomfortable.

Yes, you would have been a good father, Luc. But I don't know if I would've been a good mother. An individual in my profession, so-to-speak. I couldn't risk it. Don't you find that amusing, the sentimental side of your wife? Mother, destroyer of worlds?

Liesbet kissed the child on the cheek, lingering close. "You are a very lucky little girl," the woman whispered. She could feel the Beth Lee's breath on her face; smell the ever-so-vague baby sourness of it. "– very few get my protection."

"... devils and the wolves." Beth's words were sleepy and tumbled out.

"– *Shh,* it's fine. I know them well."

Liesbet remembered her fear of becoming a mother and the way she'd ended that possibility the night she ran to the town and Cleys Pub. The weather much like her first visit. Such a strong memory: the wind and the cold numbing her face, the snow blowing sideway in the sky. She couldn't stay pregnant, couldn't bring a child into their lives. Her plan was to protect their baby by not having it. *A baby not born, can't be murdered,* she had thought. That night the men at Cleys Pub bought her drinks and joked with her. Liesbet knew what to do with men – how to stir them, how to cause a fight or two. Let a couple of these men go home early and complain to their wives. Spread the news. Let them talk it up, the way friends were fighting friends, good men, decent men, all because of some wicked creature poisoning their trust – that Grendel woman.

Liesbet had gotten her wish.

"Foul, she was," Hendryk Verhoeven had told his Mrs. "Vulgar – that's what any Christian would say, and rightly true." Hendryk owned the bakery near the pub. A man who was big in his shoulder and belly, his white hair tied off in the back. "You should have seen her, going from this one to that one. An evil thing just ready to cause trouble. Whispering secrets. Laughing. Letting them touch her, too – whatever part interested."

"– That Grendel witch," The wife said to herself.

Hendryk's wife was short and had a round face with red, cold-weathered cheeks and chin. She'd been one of the women who had stoned Liesbet Grendel no more than two months ago.

"Her, exactly," the baker said.

"And you'd be an innocent in all that?"

"I'm here. Isn't your husband home?"

"Learning comes slow to some," Mrs. Verhoeven said.

The night ended with nine of the town's women dragging Liesbet behind Cleys Pub and stoning her. What she had wanted, wasn't it? But Liesbet didn't think it would happen so soon and with such rage.

A LARGE POMEGRANATE tree was not too far from where Liesbet Grendel sat in the Jardin Botanico. Morning sunshine filtered through the leaves and branches and speckled the woman in yellow light.

"– Mrs. Grendel?"

"– Yes?"

"I'm Annie Silva."

"I know, dear."

"So you know why I'm here."

"– Sit down." Mrs. Grendel patted the spot beside her on the wood bench. Annie didn't move. The woman paused a moment; then said, "Come on. I'm old. If you stand like that, I'll get a crick in my neck."

"I'm not interested in your neck."

Liesbet looked past Annie and toward the street. She had no expression, or none Annie could recognize – patient and waiting, perhaps. Traffic on the Paseo del Prado was less congested than earlier in the morning but vehicles still weaved about for the better lane, occasionally honking at one another.

Annie sat on the opposite end of the bench.

"– A little closer," Mrs. Grendel said. When Annie finally obliged – easing in a few inches – the woman turned to her and smiled. "Good, very good. See, we're getting along already. I have something of yours. Valuable and irreplaceable, no doubt. I can see why, too. The child can certainly steal a heart. *And* – you have something of mine, more than one thing, really."

"The Grendel painting and the diary."

"What an intelligent girl."

"You are that Grendel, aren't you? His wife?" Annie didn't wait for a reply. "I don't know how you could be."

"– The Flemish girl next door?" Liesbet grinned, her teeth small, even and very white.

"Whatever, yes. But that definitely wouldn't be you." Morning sunshine went through the branches of the nearby pomegranate tree and flickered across Annie's eyes. She had to squint and cup her hand above her brow to stop the light. "So how does a person do that? You can't be from his time, Luc Grendel's time. And I can't imagine you being from mine."

"Perhaps your attention should be focused on Beth Lee."

"I think Grendel met you on those steps, didn't he? The steps in his painting. Somehow he did that."

"You have a lot to consider," Liesbet said, ignoring the question. "I'm sure you agree. My things aren't as precious as a child's life, of course. What is, am I right? A painting, a diary, nothing compares to that little girl. But my things are precious and irreplaceable to me."

"You want us to trade."

"– Very bright." The woman was gazing out at the traffic.

14

The rented Jet and the Café
Madrid

On what to do with Mrs. Grendel

THE CESSNA CITATION was cruising at forty-three thousand feet. The pilot had just announced they were seventeen minutes away from the Madrid-Barajas Airport. The aircraft couldn't have been more steady, more silent. Taylor Bane had to look out the window to make sure they were actually in the air and cruising at roughly 600 mph. He'd picture a dark stealth bomber slipping through the sky with barely a breath. Then there was fuckin Eddy. Eddy had thrown up twice.

"You can't feel it move," Taylor said, meaning the Cessna. "How do you get sick, for Christ-sake."

"I got an imagination."

"– Yeah, you got something."

"That's what Bailey's mother said."

They both laughed at that. Taylor had picked Eddy over Bailey for the trip. He had done this for two reasons. One, Bailey was a pain in the ass. Two, Eddy could kill puppies and still be an amusing son of a bitch.

"The situation doesn't feel right," Taylor said, fingering his tie. He was wearing his white cotton suit and shirt. This was the attire he thought most about when he thought about Madrid in the summer –he thought bullfights, the sun, sweating, sangria and whites suits. Then Taylor said, “I’m getting bad feelings.”

“We’ll take care of it.”

“I have concerns with the Grendel woman. I’ve looked into it, called some people. She’s not liked. Nothing specific. She’s simply not liked. The consensus is, Grendel hires *you* but you pay *her*. I have a similar feeling. This is what happens when

I trust others.”

“– You mean Bailey.”

“I’m too trusting,” Taylor said, as if disillusioned by his better nature. “Even friends make mistakes.”

“Forget Grendel. She bleeds, yeah?”

“Who knows what she does.”

“We’ve always taken care of it,” Eddy said. “That’s why you have me, what you pay me to do.”

“Why am I not comforted?”

They were sitting in soft gray leather chairs. In front of them, a matching marble top table was draped in a cream-colored cloth. Cool lavender-scented air wafted about the Citation’s cabin from unseen vents. On the table was a bottle of Krug 1990 in a silver Queen Anne champagne bucket.

Eddy was on his third glass.

“You trust me, right?” Eddy said and took another sip.

Taylor stared out the window and stayed quiet

“Hey, boss. It’s me.” Eddy waited for a response but when none came, he said,

“We’ve known each other since high school. We’re fraternity brothers. Am I right?

You tell me what to do, I do it.”

Taylor Bane continued looking out the window of the Cessna. “Shit, you’d kill me if you had the chance.”

“You pay me too good for that.”

Taylor considered this and nodded. "– Okay, that part's true."

"Sure it is. Sure." Eddy had on his pressed jeans and a tan leather sport jacket. The sales woman had told him the jacket was made from the "very finest baby lambs." Eddy had always liked that. "You know what I think? I think if I'd shot the Silva girl myself, we wouldn't be having this conversation."

Now Bane did turn from the window to look at him, stared for a second or so. "This is why you shouldn't think. You don't understand motive. Cops do nothing but look for motive. It's all about the motive. So who has more of a motive to kill Annie Silva – a middle-aged woman, or the three guys who raped her and her buddy?"

"– Us?"

"Very good. A regular Einstein."

"THE WOMAN WHO has been hired to kill you..." Annie remembering what Winifred Bane had told her, the woman whispering through the entire conversation for fear she'd be overheard: "...her name is Grendel. Okay? Can you hear that? Liesbet Grendel."

"You mean like the painter?"

"I don't know painters. I'm saying it's Grendel."

"There's a painter named Grendel." The connection was bad and Annie had to shout this into the phone. "Is the name like that Grendel?"

Freddie didn't know painters. She knew a name.

Annie was sitting under a big leafy oak at her favorite café in the Plaza de Santa Ana. The afternoon was warm and bright. Thankfully a large tree shaded her table, and a decent enough breeze would come and go. She'd ordered a half carafe of the red and had been sipping on her second glass for maybe fifteen minutes. Annie was reading the last few pages of the Grendel diary, one leg tucked under her, the wine glass in her left hand. She still wore her floppy brimmed straw hat and sunglasses. To conceal herself, mostly. *Oh look it's the sick girl having wine. Hi, sick girl, why aren't you working?* Being at the café at this time of the day was like cutting classes in high school. She and Mariel used to do that *all* the time, but particularly during the spring.

"You do realize the two of us could get ourselves fired?" Fr. Rafa sat down in the chair across from her and pantomimed a drinking motioned to his usual waiter. "– Let's hope God forgives the occasional afternoon vodka."

"Thank you for coming."

"I'm as concerned about this as you are," he said. "To think of something terrible happening to that child – well, it's more than I'd care to imagine." A breeze moved the leaves and branches above them. Then the warm air became gusty, blowing about the friar's dark thinning hair. His fingers smoothed the strands as he talked. "You should go to the policia. I've told you that. This is serious business."

"Don't scold."

"I'm not scolding. I'm just saying –"

"I need a friend, Rafa. Be my friend."

"You're risking the child's life."

"– My life, too. Me *and* Beth." Annie closed the Grendel diary and placed in her leather handbag. "Don't have me regret calling you. Be a friend, be a person. Why is that so impossible for you?"

Fr. Rafa didn't answer.

He folded his hands on the table and looked down at them. He seemed ashamed, maybe embarrassed. Who knew with him. *Talk about scolding someone,* Annie thought. *Just beat the guy up, why don't you.*

The waiter came, left the vodka martini and moved on to other tables. Right away the friar took a sip and followed that up with a second. He held the glass, his little finger pointing out. The finger was trembling.

The woman is here to kill me," Annie said, the first time out loud. She felt her stomach go tight.

"How do you know that?"

"I know that."

"But *how* do–"

"– *Not* your business. I *know*." Annie stopped, closed her eyes for a moment and tried to calm herself. "If I help Liesbet Grendel, maybe Beth will be okay. If I don't help her – or go to the policia, we'll both be in shit. And that's about it. I don't *have* good options. I have options that are less horrible that other options."

"What does Grendel want, exactly?"

THE SEAT BELT sign had just blinked, followed by a muted *bing!* The Citation was preparing to land at Madrid-Barajas. Taylor and Eddy took at last sips of the Krug 1990 and buckled their harnesses. Taylor looked out the small window. He never liked thinking about the plane leaving the ground but he did like watching the plane land, especially the feeling of the wheels meeting the runway.

"Tell me what do," Eddy said.

"Have another drink."

"You know what I mean."

Taylor leaned back in the Citation's over-sized gray leather seat. He stared at Eddy, hesitating before he said, "You'll go where she's staying. You'll introduce yourself, discuss our concerns."

"Where is she staying?"

"– Just be quiet right now. Let me finish. Can you do that?" Taylor hated losing his temper with the guy.

Eddy was his favorite but when Taylor thought about it, Eddy and Bailey were both assholes, each in their own unique way. "You're polite with her, a gentleman. Are you listening?"

"Yes I'm listening. Of course."

"You represent me, Edward – not that you mention my name, okay? You don't ever mention my name. But you enquire. *Discreetly,* you enquire. 'My employer is interested in knowing where we are on that project,' you say. 'Perhaps an estimate. How soon will you be completing our contract?' See what I mean? But in your own words. This is simply the attitude you should have – a gentleman, not a thug. And discreet, always that. Discreet."

Taylor felt the vibration of the Cessna's engines reversing themselves for the landing. Automatically, he gripped the armrests.

"– And if she doesn't," Eddy said.

"Doesn't what?" Who has a conversation when the plane is landing? Taylor shut his eyes.

"The Grendel woman – if she doesn't cooperate."

"We'll reassess."

"You mean shoot her."

"What did I just say? We are *al*ways –what?"

"So discreetly shoot her?"

AFTERNOON SUNLIGHT BLINKED in and out of thick dark clouds. The air had become cooler and the breezes had grown stronger and more frequent, fluttering the leaves of the nearby oak. Annie and Fr. Rafa were sitting at the small café table in the Plaza de Santa Ana. The friar had finished his first martini and had begun another. Annie was on her last half glass of red from the carafe.

"I can't do that," Fr. Rafa said, waving a dismissive hand far too broadly. The vodka had already reached his motor skills. Annie had told him that Liesbet Grendel wanted both the painting and the diary in exchange for Beth Lee.

"You have to help me," She said. Her sunglasses had slipped to the edge of her nose and she pushed the glasses back with a forefinger. "I know you won't let

Grendel hurt this child."

"You're asking me to steal."

"I'm asking you to help save a *person*." Annie sounded both desperate and angry. *A pleading, angry shrew,* her self-appraisal. "I've seen you with Beth. You like her, I know you. Don't tell me different."

"It has nothing to do with me liking her."

"It has everything to do with you liking her." She reached for the carafe and poured the last of the red into her glass. After a quick swallow, she said, "No, no, wait that's not true. Even if you *didn't* like her – even if you thought she was the most horrid little girl you had ever met – she is still someone who needs your help. And that's what you do, right? Isn't that what you people do?"

"– Excuse me. 'You *people*'?"

"Hey, don't get all indignant. You know perfectly well what I meant, okay? Let me rephrase: it's your *calling* or whatever, what you *do*. Unless you're all show and no go. Is that it, friar? Show but no go?"

Fr. Rafa had a sip of his martini then placed the glass precisely in front him. "Even if I said yes. Which I'm not – and let me tell you that right now, young lady, I most unequivocally am *not* – I'd need a *lot* of detail."

Annie Silva shut her eyes when she heard the "young lady" thing. The friar was at least ten years younger than her. She thought, *You pompous little shit.* But she kept quiet. Annie bit the side of her cheek, the metallic taste of blood on the probing tip of her tongue. She didn't want to alienate the friar. He was already half paralyzed by just the idea of stealing the painting – that and the martini.

Rafa had another sip of his drink, a bigger sip than the last. "Suppose I were to consider your...scheme," he said. The word "plan" seemed too normal. "How do you walk out of the museum with a painting that's close to five feet high and –what? – four feet wide?"

"– Five-three and a half by four-one and a quarter," Annie said. "And you cover it and walk out. Paintings come and go all the time, Rafa. I know you know that. What you don't do is leave an empty space. People who drop by the studio should see me working on it."

"Worse, still. How does one do that?"

"We replace it with another painting."

The friar rubbed his middle finger along the rip of the martini glass. "And this 'other' painting – we would get that where?"

"– From me. My painting."

"*Your* painting?" the friar said. The disbelief in his tone bordered on a smirk. "You do understand my hesitation. My skepticism, to be blunt. Not only would you need to have the talent of Grendel, you'd have to paint in his style. Then there is the matter of the paint – the pigments of that period, that sort of thing. No, you couldn't pull that off."

"It's better than the original." Annie finished off the red and set the wine glass next to the empty carafe. "If you're thinking I'd planned to steal the Grendel all along, I wasn't. Blame me painting the copy on my obsessive nature but don't blame my motive.

All I wanted to do was a good job so the museum would hire me for other projects."

"I'll need to see the painting."

"It's being delivered. Mrs. Grendel said after five. My building manager agreed to let her leave it in my apartment." Annie glanced at her watch. "– Two hours and some minutes, so come over. My place. I'll give you Free milk and cookies."

"Does the Prado know?" The friar swallowed the last of his drink, too. "Did you show them the picture?"

"I already *had* the job, Rafa. I did the painting strictly for me."

Wind gusted up and bits of grit from the plaza stung Annie's face. She pressed

the top of her floppy brim hat against her head. Strands of Fr. Rafa's dark thinning hair whipped at his forehead. People sitting close to Annie and the friar tried to hold down their plates and drinks. One woman squealed when a napkin leaped away from the table and fluttered above her like an oddly shaped white bird. Then the wind stopped as abruptly as it had started.

"I don't understand," the friar said. "How does the woman get this painting to you so soon and with such good timing? How can someone promise that?"

"I'm guessing she's been planning this for a while."

15

In the apartments of Annie and Liesbet
Madrid

Surprises from the Plaza Mayor

THE PAINTING HAD startled Annie. She'd walked into her apartment and there it was in front of the fold out black lacquered divider that separated the living area from the bed area. *Meeting on the steps to Hades* had been set on a new dark wood easel. Polished mahogany, probably. A second or two had passed before Annie realized the work was her copy of the Grendel Painting, the one *she* had painted. The easel must have been a gift from the woman who'd had the picture sent from Annie's home in Brentwood.

"How did you do that?" Annie had asked Liesbet Grendel yesterday in the Jardin

Botanico. Mrs. Grendel had just said that Annie's painting shipped a week ago from her home by Big Ben Silva, Annie's dad.

"What a truly *charm*ing man," Mrs. Grendel said. Annie had hated the thick and oppressive morning heat– she'd felt the sweat on her back and under her arms – but the woman looked fresh and cool, even with the white cape. Then Mrs. Grendel said, "I told your father I worked at the Prado. I told him how busy you'd been and that you needed the painting sent to your apartment. Basically, that was my entire message – the rest was chit-chat. We must have talked for thirty or forty minutes. Your father adores you, you know."

"Yeah, I know." Annie didn't like the woman talking about her father like the two of them were all buddy-buddy.

God this is going to happen. I'm going to steal a painting. I'm going to become a thief. The idea was both sexy and horrible at the same time.

The skylights and large windows in Annie's apartment revealed a cloudy late afternoon and the runny clear lines of a previous rain lay motionless on the glass. The apartment walls were cluttered with enlarged photographs she had taken of Luc Grendel's painting. No frames, no order to it – just photos attached to the walls with tape and metal tacks. Annie let her leather handbag drop to the floor beside her; dropped the floppy brim straw hat and sunglasses, too. She hadn't quit staring at the painting, studying it. A good painting. Passable, very passable. It could go unnoticed, particularly on her easel in the Prado's conservation studio.

No one goes in there. No one would see the painting except Rafa and me. Worse case: I could get two, three days out of it, maybe a week...before they'd catch me, before they'd figure out what happened.

That would be time enough.

Annie knelt, opened her handbag and found Luc Grendel's diary. She stood and pressed the diary to her chest, as if it had the power to protect her.

SHE'D OFFERED HIM ice tea and told him, "Please, sit. We don't need to be all formal to discuss business." Eddy had told Mrs. Grendel that his visit had to do with the contract between her and his employer. The woman pointed to the worn red velour chair in the corner of the room. He said no thanks to the tea but he sat in the chair and crossed his legs at the knee, brushing off an invisible something from his tan chinos. First impression: the woman seemed very welcoming, very nice. Eddy hadn't known what to expect from her. He certainly hadn't expected "nice." *I don't see the fuckin problem,* he thought.

"Who's in the bed?" Eddy nodded toward the other side of the room at the small misshaped mound covered by a white sheet.

"I'm looking after a sick child," the woman whispered and put a finger to her lips. "– For a friend. Poor things, both of them – the mother and the child. Our girl's a very sound sleeper but it's best we don't raise our voices. We don't want to disturb the dear."

Charitable, too. No, Eddy didn't see the problem.

Sun appeared between the many clouds of an earlier rain. The light was muted and silver and came through the open doors of the balcony and across the wood floor, the bed area and the child lost to shadows.

"You're Mr. Bane's man, aren't you?" the woman said.

"I'm here discuss your contract." Eddy remembered what Taylor had told him. *You represent me, Edward – not that you mention my name, okay? You don't ever mention my name.*

"– To check on me?"

"– To discuss the contract. Your progress."

"Most people would call that checking on a person." She wouldn't let it go.

Okay, maybe she is a fuckin problem.

The other thing Taylor said, *A gentleman, not a thug. And discreet, always that. Discreet.*

"You're right," Eddy said to the woman, big grin; playing it like a gentleman and a scholar. No, better than that, much better than that, like one of those suave guys in the old movies. Cary Grant, maybe. "You got my number, Missus."

"Oh do I?" Liesbet Grendel giving Eddy her flirty voice as she seated herself on the pale blue Victoria couch opposite him. Her cape covered her shoulders and arms and draped over her knees. Underneath the cape and strapped to her left arm was the leather sheath that held the pick with the pearl handle. "Well I'm sure we both have each other's number, don't we?"

Eddy held up the palms of his hands. "I'm just the messenger."

"Me, too." She smiled again.

Both the couch and the chair were very old and the sunlight showed worn backs and armrests. When she first sat on the couch, a fine sunlit dust poofed out from the cushion and now hovered about her. "So we're messengers, you and I. Who would've thought such a thing – us having similar callings, so-to-speak. I wonder what else we have in common?"

"I'm guessing not too much," Eddy said. He was looking past the woman and toward the shadowy bed area and the sleeping child. "Take me, I'm a procrastinator. That's all I do – procrastinate. I was that way in college. If I had a term paper due, you could be sure I'd start that paper on the last night. Don't get me wrong, I would always finish my work. Still do. But it would take me all night." Eddy turned and studied the woman. "Are you like that, Missus? Do you procrastinate?"

"I've never been a college girl."

"That wasn't my question."

THERE WERE ONLY two and a half pages left in the Grendel diary. Annie was sitting in the salmon colored wingback near a window that looked down on the

Calle Ruiz de Alarcon. Even on this cloudy day, the skylights and windows brought more than enough light into her apartment. She was waiting to show her painting to Fr. Rafa – and he was late, the man was always late – so she'd begun reading the final pages of the diary and the last part surprised her. Here and only here, Luc Grendel spoke directly to his new bride.

WOENSDAG, 1567

You do not fool me. You will steal my painting and you will steal this diary. I refuse to hide them, of course. I cannot go through life hiding what is valuable to me from the woman I love. That is not how I want to live. When you finally read this diary - and I am sure you will, read it more than once probably, read it and hate me for it - you will know both my suspicions about you and my love for you. Yes, take the painting, take the diary. That is what you want, isn't it? To disappear from my life. To steal every clue that you ever knew me, that you and I ever loved each other? Don't say I'm wrong. You and I know how right I am. It doesn't matter that I would never hurt you, that I am foolish enough to love you always. You won't allow a bit of this to get in the way of your rage. I have not seen anyone embrace anger the way you do. So cold, so overwhelmed by what you have called my "betrayal." How dare I paint the dream and the world you took me to see. <u>Betrayal</u> - You say the word as if as if I had declared your worse secret to everyone then taken the knife to you.

Liesbet, you do not fool me. Go on - leave our life, our bed. Toss it, lie about, say it meant nothing. Say it was an amusement. Isn't that what you told me amid one tantrum or another? "You are merely an amusement, Luc, a way to tolerate this world."

I am a painter.

What did you expect me to do? Think about that, sweet dear. You revealed wonders I could have never imagined. Never. And I am very good at imagining so many things. You've let me see a world other than this one. Taunted me with more. How did you put it? Your words to me, "I could not count all the worlds I have seen, Luc, darling."

That stole my breath, you know. When you said, "I could not count all the worlds –" the air in the room vanished. Poof! Like that. We went outside the cabin so I could calm myself. Remember? I had to stand in the open air just to breathe again.

You didn't let up, though –on and on you went – a smile at the corners of your mouth. "I've seen Caesar walk the streets of Rome," you had said. "I have seen Christ call to his father on the cross."

You know what I thought?

Take me with you.

I thought, my God what I could see, what I could paint. The flood, the temptation, the building of the pyramids, the possibilities left me weak.

Still, they leave me weak.

Oh, Liesbet. My dear, my sweet. I can picture your anger as you read my words. "Not only does this wretched painter betray me, you say, "but he cares more for these worlds than he does for me."

Why can I not love you and want to see those times, those places? Maybe this is what we were meant to do, you and I. Yes, I believe it's true. Consider the wondrous life we'd spend together as we travel through worlds. Have you thought that?

I cannot change your nature; nor can you change mine. Ask the fox not to hunt; expect the homing pigeon to forget his home - it can't be done. I haven't always known what you do, Liesbet, but I have known it for a while. It's a job usually left to passionate acts and armies of all sorts and causes. But you are neither hero or villain. Nor would I call you desperate, and certainly not spurned. Perhaps there are personal benefits, say, the way one would prove his worth to an employer or a group, I don't know.

You are a mystery and a category unto yourself, Liesbet, unique and with motives I couldn't begin to understand. And, yes, you are more dangerous because of that. Who could fathom the rules you go by, the world that gave them to you?

But the heart is not logical, is it?

The heart yearns, it feels, it knows its power and leaves all tired and fretting thoughts to the mind.

Hear me now, Liesbet. Read me carefully.

I have this to say to you - my pledge to you, my guarantee - bring back the painting and the diary, dearest, and I will say no more of it. All will be forgotten.

Yes, it will be as if none of it occurred.

Oh I can hear you now. "This is not about <u>you</u>, Luc. You betrayed <u>me</u>. I did nothing to you. You painted another world for everyone to see, my world. This was for you and me, only. I trusted you with my secret. I trusted you to keep me safe."

I don't expect you to come to me right away. Let the years pass; let time walk you as slowly as it wishes. You have shown me there are more worlds than this one, and I am waiting for you in mine. I can see you now: I will be out back in the meadow painting and you will appear to me the way you did the first time.

And we will begin again.

"SO YOU'RE AN assassin, too?" Liesbet wanted to know. She said the question as if it was another thing they had in common – like two strangers with the same school ring, or the habit of wearing shoes without socks.

"My employer is concerned," Eddy said, ignoring her question. He sat in the faded red velour chair in a shadowed corner of Mrs. Grendel's apartment. "At the risk of sounding like my mother, you don't call, you don't write. We have to track you down simply to find out how you're doing. God that *does* sound like my mother."

"You didn't answer my question."

"I don't have to," Eddy said.

"That doesn't seem fair."

"Let's just say 'fair' is over-rated."

"I'm trying to get to know you." She gave him her best pouty face. A person would've thought she was disappointed, maybe even a little heartbroken.

"Forgive me, Mrs. Grendel, but you have a way of confusing the rules." Eddy's legs were crossed, folded hands propped on his knee. He had on chinos and a nice blue button-down, nothing fancy. *Be a regular person with her*, that was the idea, *everyone comfortable, everyone talking*. That shit never works. "See we're paying you money. A large sum of money.

We don't answer questions. But you have an obligation to answer ours."

"This is a trust issue, isn't it?"

"– Yeah, sort of." Eddy never knew if the woman was kidding or not. She talked like every situation was a joke and only she knew the punchline.

Mrs. Grendel walked to the balcony and looked down at the square below and the surround buildings of the Plaza Mayor. Then she glanced at the bed area and the child. There were shadows but she could see Beth Lee's blue cotton cap and the tiny shape of her under the white sheet.

"My memory isn't good," she said, still looking at the child.

"I'm guessing it's fine."

"I don't recall a time frame in our agreement." Now Mrs. Grendel turned and looked at him. No expression, no hints. "– A particular date. A particular hour. That sort of thing, nothing about particulars."

"Do you intend to fulfill your contract?"

"What weapon do you use, Eddy?"

"– Excuse me?"

"– Pistol, knife? Brass knuckles – do you beat them to death?"

"I use a Beretta PX4 Storm compact."

"You got it on you?"

Fuck her. "I always got it on me."

"– Thought as much." Liesbet sat on the edge of the bed and began to stroke the sleeping child's cheek with the back of a finger. She kissed Beth's forehead. "Tell me," she whispered to Eddy, "Where do you keep this Beretta? You don't wear a jacket or a sportscoat coat."

"I never pictured you as the caregiver type," he said, watching Grendel with the

child.

"– You tuck it in the back?" she said. "The gun, I mean."

The man lifted his right pant leg. The Beretta was strapped to his thin white calf.

"– Satisfied?" he said.

"You pull up your pants to shoot somebody?"

Before Eddy could respond to her, Liesbet Grendel had left the bed, crossed the room and circled behind him in a motion so fluid and immediate that Eddy thought she'd left the room.

He first felt the blood come up in the back of his throat then he felt an area of unbearable pain the size of his fingertip at the back of his neck. Blood began flooding his open mouth and spilling down his blue button shirt. He had also heard something in the back of his neck crack. *Shit...God, shit.* He tried his best to turn and see the woman but nothing worked – arms, legs, a simple twist of the torso – nothing worked.

He couldn't even get himself to scream.

16

Mundo 24 Horas, Conversatorios
Madrid

Taylor Bane does a TV interview

"I MET YOUR friend," the woman on his cell said.

"What friend? Who is this?"

"You know perfectly well who this is."

He didn't have time for mystery shit. Fifteen minutes before his interview on Mundo 24 Horas, Taylor Bane was sitting in a black leather and chrome swivel chair getting his hair combed by a semi-hot lady who reminded him of Freddie, particularly the legs. The TV studio was dark except for a single lighted bulb near the makeup tray. Before Taylor had answered the persistent hum of his cell – and heard the *other* one, the woman with the mystery shit – he'd told the semi-hot lady with the legs how he was tight with the Hispanics in California. The lovely lady told him she was from Sao Paulo and liked thinking of herself as a Latino.

"Having cultural issues, are we?" the woman on his cell said. Very amused, very

what would you call it? Cuntlike.

"Wait. I got to take this call." Taylor waved away the Latino-Hispanic-whatever,

irritated now – truly irritated – and whispered to the woman on the phone, "You've got thirty seconds. Who are you?"

"– The one with the contract."

"– *You*. Grendel, isn't it?"

"Such a charmer."

"Let me talk to Eddy."

"Eddy can't come to the phone."

"I pay him. He'll come to the phone."

"– Not this time." Her words were followed by a dial tone.

TAYLOR THOUGHT THE interview would give him international cred; also cred with the Hispanics who were becoming the largest ethnic group in his state. In five more years, Hispanics would account for 40.7 percent of California while good ole white

boys would be at 36.4 percent. Which really ticked off a lot of good ole white boys. So getting on the ground floor of the whole Hispanic thing was important.

"You are very popular with Hispanics in America," the interviewer said. Andreo Mattos was slim and young with dark-framed glasses and neatly parted hair. He wore a skinny cream-colored suit and a blue shirt and matching tie. He had a bit of an accent but his English was impeccable. "I get the feeling Hispanics have a friend in Taylor Bane."

"– Well for sure California Hispanics. Not that I don't have a fondness and respect for all my Hispanic friends."

"We forget how big America is, yes?"

"Big, bold and beautiful," said Taylor and gave Andreo and the TV camera what his mother often called "the winning Bane grin."

The studio lights were unbelievably hot and the air conditioning was unbelievably cold. He could imagine a collision of extremes producing a thunderstorm over camera three.

He hated fucking TV.

The interview on Mondo 24was Bailey's idea. "– Solidify the Hispanic vote," he'd said. "Taylor Bane goes to the Old Country, very good stuff. Then we get their sister station to replay the interview here in Los Angeles. You can't beat the coverage.

It's like being a senator from New York visiting Israel."

"They got a sister station in LA?"

"– Like Telemundo on steroids."

Okay, occasionally Bailey has a good idea. Taylor didn't mind giving credit if credit was due. Of course he could've asked Bailey why they didn't do the goddamn interview in goddamn LA. *But the Grendel woman wasn't in LA, was she*? He could hear Bailey saying this in that douchebag way of his. Again he'd be right. This wasn't just about an interview, this was about a woman who didn't want to do her job, a job Taylor Bane was paying her to do – or in this case, not do. And he didn't like being played. Who does? Even the hint of being played put a knot in his stomach the size of a softball. The Grendel woman was here in Madrid acting like the people around her were blundering little peons – including Taylor Bane, that's what *truly* pissed him off. What do you call a person who gives another person money to do a job and all the other person does is avoid the job and treats her employer with disrespect? A *schmuck* is what you call him, a loser, dirt beneath the shoe, a person who doesn't deserve respect.

Andreo Mattos had asked Taylor another a question. His fifth or sixth question, Taylor couldn't remember. Mattos was becoming a jerk very, very quickly – him in his tight faggy suit and his pointy shoes – but Taylor tried to focus.

"– You were a teenager then?"

"I'm sorry. What?"

Andreo gave the widest toothy grin Taylor Bane had ever seen. The boy had some big teeth. "I can see why you might not want to hear me. I said, 'Tell me about when you and your friends raped those two teenage girls – 'allegedly' raped. It was never proven, yes?"

"I HAVE A man in Madrid who comes in and cleans," the woman said. This was how she answered the phone – no "hello," no "who is this?" She opens with her cleaner, her voice calm, matter-of-fact.

The last caller on Taylor Bane's cell was Eddy, or Eddy's number. Taylor had requested a break from Mattos and his questions. He wanted to punch Andreo Mattos in the throat but knew he had to maintain. He had to stay and finish; walking away would have shown guilt. So Taylor went for second best. He took a piss break and called Eddy's number.

The woman on his cell was saying, "– I've used this gentleman a few times in the past. I recommend him. Very detailed, very professional."

"– Is Eddy dead?" Taylor whispered. He was by himself in the men's room,

staring at his own disbelief in the mirror above the marble sink.

"Let's say he's gone."

"What do you mean – *gone*?"

"Gone as in gone. Not here."

"– As in dead?"

"My man is very thorough," the woman said. She could have been talking about anyone who provided a service, the gardener, the pool boy, anyone. Her manner stayed relaxed, even friendly. "He cleans the furniture, the rug, whatever was touched," she said. "He takes care of ...well everything, really. You just walk away knowing the entire matter will be dealt with efficiently, effectively. *And* it's a family business – imagine – I love that idea. Don't you love that? People who have pride in what they do? So European. This is the fourth generation, you know."

"Answer the question."

"– But listen to me. You must know about such things." The woman paused, no more than a beat or two, enough to let her words be magnified by the silence. "You must have people who – what do we call it? – *assist* you in this or that. The ones who are there to tidy up, so-to-speak. I mean sooner or later we must learn to rely on others. Now I'm not talking about throwing caution to the wind, of course. You can't trust every so-n-so who passes by, that would be foolish. I surely wouldn't do that; you wouldn't, either. But within a certain parameter – *chosen* others. And once you've chosen this person or that one, you stick with it and you stand back. If you have to learn how to stand back, you learn it. You stand back. But your fuse, Mr. Em*ploy*er, your fuse for trusting is way too short."

"Eddy was that person," Bane said. "What did you call it, the chosen other?"

"Yes, he was. So am I."

"And look what happened."

"Who's fault is that?"

TAYLOR BANE had seated himself in the black leather and chrome chair across from Andreo who was busy pinning his microphone back onto the lapel of his cream-colored suitcoat. He gave Taylor his big Nothing But Teeth grin. The Tungsten lights above them were intensely bright and hot but Andreo could have been sitting in an air-conditioned bar on Calle Amirante, his hair perfect, not a drop of perspiration.

Taylor felt the dampness under his arms and on his neck and shoulders, and he wondered how the guy did it.

"– Welcome back to *Conversatorios*." Andreo said this to the camera just over Bane's left shoulder. "Before the break we were discussing our guest's – what would you call your younger days? – 'turbulent'?"

"What young person's life isn't turbulent?

"But *your* life then, what would you call it?"

"– Average, I guess. I don't know." Taylor's legs were crossed and his hands were folded and propped on his thigh. He'd become aware that the left hand was a tight fist, and the right hand was hiding it. "Your universities, they have fraternities. Young boys – *men* – young *men* who like having a good time. Maybe they drink too much at a party. Get a little crazy. I don't know, whatever they do nowadays. Doesn't that happen here?"

"Boys will be boys?"

"– that's it, yes."

"Does that include rape?"

Andreo Mattos waited for an answer. The camera over Andreo's right shoulder glided silently toward Taylor, who head was bowed as if offering a prayer.

"I'm appreciative of what you said in the beginning of our conversation," Bane said. He kept his voice controlled, casual. His smile didn't waver. *This fucker isn't the only one who knows how to smile.* Then in his Nixonian third person, "Taylor Bane *is* a friend to Hispanics. I want the Hispanic community here and in California to know that their issues are my issues. I can promise that right now, unequivocally." He looked directly at the camera, his smile gone, his demeanor earnest. "Listen to me, every one of you. This is my promise to my Hispanic friends in

California–solving your issues will be my last thought at night and my first thought in the morning. Any hint – and I mean *any* hint – of a second-class citizenry is simply and rightly unacceptable. Period, end of story. If I have the honor to serve as senator, I'll fight for the Hispanics who vote for me and the ones who didn't. It won't matter, I'll be your senator, too. Whether it's a legal pathway to citizenship – tough but *always* fair – or to end discrimination in the workplace, in housing, you name it, I'll stand with you. That I can promise."

When Taylor Bane had finished, he looked down at his lap, his folded hands, the palm of one covering the fist of the other. *If you're going to be attacked, make sure you let people know what side you're on. Okay, kiddo. Have a go.* He waited for Mattos but heard nothing except the vague hum of the studio's air conditioning. He felt the heat of the lights on the back of his neck. Finally Taylor looked up and tried to figure Andreo's expression – a sadness in the eyes, a kindness edged in empathy. *The guy's good. He'll have them believing I've broken his heart.* Taylor felt his chances to become a senator were about to be undone.

"I'm sure your dedication is genuine," Andreo Mattos said, the words soft but not whispered, the concern gentle but not condescending, that balance of sincere caring and potential earthquake that seemed at the core of Andreo's talent. "Forgive a young man, Mr. Bane. I'm a skeptic, I know. I am part of this jaded media –a card carrying member of that very suspicious group –it's my downfall. There are days I believe I am nothing but an amusement to my viewers, what few viewers I have left."

"– You exaggerate, Mr. Mattos."

"– A dispassionate, truthful look at myself, Mr. Bane." Andreo waited for Bane to have a sip from his glass of water and return the glass to the small coffee table between them. "We have a saying in Spain, '*Saber que una persona debe conocer su pasado.*' To know a person is to know his past. Have you heard of it?"

Definitely out of my depth.

"But what of transformation, Andreo." *Beat him to his question, head him off. I need to take charge of this.* "How many of your viewers – forgive me, perhaps even yourself – regret some part of their youth, some impetuous moment they'd take back if only they could?

"– Impetuous." Mattos hesitated, contemplating the word, allow it to simmer and descend into the ether. "That's an interesting word choice. Impetuous. Like getting a speeding ticket? Would that be impetuous?"

"I suppose, yes."

"– Getting drunk with one's friends."

"– We can all relate to that." Taylor laughed and hoped it sounded innocent and good natured. But he also heard the nervousness in it. "Certainly Yours Truly can relate. How 'bout you, Andreo?"

"Drunk with school friends? Of course."

"Well there you go." Taylor felt the muscles in his stomach start to relax.

"Does being impetuous include rape?"

THE HOTEL RITZ Madrid was next to the Prado on the Plaza De La Lealtad. Taylor Bane had told the limo driver to take his time. He needed a moment or two to think, to get himself together. Plan how to right the boat, so-to-speak. Bane needed to contain the Mondo 24 nightmare. He dictated a voice note: "Tell Bailey to cancel the

LA rebroadcast." The tension in the muscles of his stomach had returned.

That's not going to work. Now it's news. I couldn't control the fucking narrative. I let it get away from me, the story, my life, everything.

"I'm not going to discuss that with you," Taylor had told the interviewer, meaning his fraternity days and what had happened after the Halloween party. "If you want to continue our talk, we'll need to go with the issues that face our Hispanic friends. Or whatever else we find reasonable."

"How do you ignore – what's the saying? – the elephant in the room?"

"I'm a middle-aged man now," Taylor said, "not a fraternity boy."

The would-be senator was sure he'd blown it, and the more Bane thought about the interview the more he understood the importance of taking care of his Annie Silva problem.

He felt the vibration of the cell against his chest and reached into the inside pocket of his suitcoat.

"– This you?" Taylor said, a single weary breath.

"You know its me."

"Eddy came there to talk with you." Bane leaned his head against the leather backrest. "He came in good faith, my representative. And my friend. I told him, 'No violence. Discuss the issue. Act like a gentleman.' So what am I supposed to do?"

"Go on with your life."

"You know better," Taylor said. "I have to do things personally now. With you. And with her."

"Then you have a situation."

17

Museo del Prado
Madrid

Annie and Rafa become thieves

SHE'D WANTED TO walk her painting through the Prado's main lobby the next morning. Wrapped in its cloth cover, who would know? Fr. Rafa said that was her guilt talking. Annie needed to get a grip.

"I understand why you want to walk through the lobby," he told her. "Switching the paintings at night makes you feel like a thief. But that's the reality, isn't it?" This was yesterday evening when he came over to look at the copy of *Meeting on the Steps to Hades* Annie had painted in California. "Think about the investigation – and there *will* be an investigation. I can hear the guards telling the policia, 'Oh yes, I remember Annie Silva walking through the lobby with a five-foot canvas covered in a cloth.' How many objects are shaped like that? At least put up a fight. The shape doesn't disappear, you know."

Okay, he had a point.

"Is the painting good enough?" She'd been fretting about her abilities as a painter

since she had walked into her apartment that afternoon and saw her work propped on the beautiful new easel.

"You're very talented," the friar said.

"So it'll do?"

"Very nicely, I think." Rafa walked about the long narrow room, examining the painting from different angles. "This canvas – linen on poplar?"

"Yes. The pigment are from that period, too."

"– *Very* nice. Why aren't you off painting somewhere?"

"Don't get sweet so fast. You'll get a cramp." She was partly joking. Too bad it was evening. Annie would've liked Fr. Rafa to see her picture with the sun coming through the skylights and the windows. "Good. Maybe I'll have a few days before they discover it's a phony."

Let's pack it up," Friar Rafa said. "My van is downstairs."

"– *Now?*"

"There's a problem?"

"I – well – I-I don't know." His matter-of-factness startled her. Annie didn't expect him to be this enthusiastic, this ready to go. Her mind became cluttered with scenarios involving art thefts and bad outcomes. "Okay, sure, tonight. Of course tonight."

"The sooner we get the child the better."

Annie agreed. Of course she'd wanted to save Mariel, too. Still felt she could have done something; hired a specialist, maybe – shit, a *shaman* – something, someone. Now Annie had another one to save, Beth Lee, save the child from Liesbet Grendel, save her from the crazy Heather Latterimer. But saved or not, sweet Beth would die the way Mariel died, the way they all die – no matter *what* a person does, no matter how hard a person tries.

Cancer is the bitch of bitches.

The drooling, ravenous queen.

People say there are genetic switches in our DNA – control on the use-to-be uncontrollable – "on" for cancer and death; "off" for living your life. That's what

Annie had heard, or read. What can we put you down for –life, death? Have mucho guilt from not being able to save your friends? How about a big tumor? Whatever self-punishment you think will work to ease your load. Fifteen or twenty years from now we'll decide which genes to switch on or off. The secret to keeping the person you love with you is knowing your switches.

Annie imagined Mariel saying: "– Just leave my switches alone," Very feistily, too. You never had to guess what Mariel was thinking.

"Don't you want to be with me?"

"You know I adore you," Mariel said, her cool, dry hand touched Annie's cheek. "But you're late, baby – your switches, your plans. You're just late. I'm too tired, too worn from it. Let me sleep."

THE FRIAR HAD borrowed a white Econoline from the museum. They would enter through the loading dock in the back, Rafa explained, and go up the back stairs to the second floor and the conservation studio.

"Two guards are on that floor," the friar said. "We have a ten to fifteen minute

window from the stairs to the studio. It should take us less than a minute, so plenty of leeway."

"The guards show up every ten to fifteen minutes?"

"I haven't timed it – you know, precisely–but I've worked evenings often enough to make an educated guess."

"... maybe we should wait."

"Beth, too?" the friar said. "Does she wait?"

That couldn't be argued. Annie needed to put away her anxiousness and do what

Grendel wanted; set it all straight. *You can't have a child snatched from you and not do everything reasonable and not so reasonable to get the child back and safe – particularly the not so reasonable.* Annie also had a clear sense of the mother. Heather Latterimer was fleeing from her child because she couldn't stand her own feeling of helplessness. *God, I know all about that,* Annie thought. *Who wants to watch their baby die? And Mrs. Latterimer is a lot of guilt looking for a person to blame.* She'd bet the first thing out of Heather's mouth would be, "*You're* responsible. *You're* the one who killed my daughter."

You're right, lady.

I can't save shit.

At 8:34PM Annie and the friar were in the stairwell and heading up to the third floor. Florescent lights glared down on metal railings and concrete steps. Annie had wanted to take the service elevator.

They were whispering back and forth.

"Guards love elevators," the friar said. "They like to ride them down to the snack machines and coffee."

"Meantime we're lugging this painting up three flights of stairs."

"Poor us."

"I'm just saying. It'd be nice."

"I saw you as more stoic," Rafa said.

"I'm nervous. I talk when I'm nervous."

Annie was holding one end of the painting, the friar the opposite end. He was

walking backwards up the steps. They continued to whisper. Occasionally Fr. Rafa would glance over his shoulder to see where he had to step next and how much further they had to go.

"You keep surprising me," Annie said. "– You helping, I mean."

"We're helping Beth."

"We're art *thieves*."

"God forgives. Trust me."

THE SECURITY PANEL next to the conservation studio door glowed blue. Fr. Rafa clicked in the code. Once inside they laid the painting against a wood work table. Windows framed the moon as it dipped in and out of clouds and put moving shadows on the white walls and cabinets. Immediately the friar put a finger to his lips and nodded toward the closed door and a footstep sound, probably the security guard.

"We can start that fifteen minutes now," he whispered.

"I don't know how criminals do it." Annie could feel the push of her heart at the sides of her neck. "The tension would kill me, but maybe it's the rush. It *is* sort of

thrilling."

"I wouldn't call Jail a thrill."

"You know what I mean. Doing something naughty."

"Naughty is showing a boy your knickers."

"– Your *what*?"

The friar pantomimed a shushing sound again.

"– *nickers*?" she whispered.

Fr. Rafa ignored her. He switched the pictures and covered the original in the cloth. Annie stepped away from her painting, studying it. A small yellow light was hooked atop the easel.

"This is *so* bad," she said, shaking her head. Then Annie walked a couple of steps toward the picture, cocked her head and squinted. "How come I didn't see these mistakes?"

"This isn't the best time to make judgments," Fr. Rafa said. He was next to the closed door, the big canvas leaning against his hip. "It's a good painting."

"But will it fool people? The powers-that-be, will it fool them?"

"For a while, yes – not forever." The friar leaned his ear to the door. "We're okay now, I think. We really need to get the original to the van." He watched her for a second, perhaps two, and smiled. "Look, Annie, it was never our intent to fool them permanently, right? We talked about this. Isn't that what we said? 'Fool them enough to get by,' was your comment, I think."

"Maybe it's not good enough for even that."

"It could be a Rembrandt, that's really not the point. We'll get caught sooner or later."

"Hey there's no 'we' here," Annie said and walked over to him. She placed her hand gently on his forearm. "You're not getting caught, I promised you that at the start. Didn't I promise you, Rafa? I'm responsible for all of this, it's my idea. As far as I'm concerned, nobody helped me. I just want us to be perfectly straight on that. It's my deal, my doing."

Getting caught wasn't the main problem, though. Annie knew there was someone else waiting for her. She hadn't forgotten Winifred Bane's phone call, and the warning: *The woman who has been hired to kill you – her name is Grendel.*

The friar continued as if he hadn't heard Annie. Maybe he didn't want to think about the Getting Caught part of it. "I'm just saying. It's not a question of 'if' we get caught. It's a question of 'when.' Hopefully the child should be okay. That's the whole point, isn't it – to get the girl back to her mother?"

"I understand that mother *so* well." Annie clicked off the small light above the easel. "I was the same with Mariel. I wanted to run away, too. Mariel who I loved more than myself, I would've absolutely abandoned her. Or some days it felt that way. Others days I hung around and annoyed the hell out of her. I couldn't stand the helpless feeling – just waiting for her to die."

"I'm glad we're doing this," Fr. Rafa said. He leaned his ear against the door again. "Okay, are you ready?"

Clouds had enveloped the moon and the white studio walls went from drifting shadows to darkness. Someone on the second floor, probably a guard, started dialing a radio through its channels – static, music, static, talk or news, more static – the radio at last settling on a female singer with an acoustical guitar. The music was coming from the far end of the hall.

Annie had been watching the friar. She thought his feelings had changed. More depressed, perhaps, she wasn't sure. "You're not getting all worried, are you?"

Rafa hesitated before he said, "– I...I envy you. I never loved anyone like that. Crazy, no holds-barred, I've never had that."

"Aren't you celibate? Isn't that what friars do?"

"We *are* human," Fr. Rafa said. "You know – *men*." A little insulted, Annie thought. Figuring Rafa was never easy. "A man doesn't have to act on each and every feeling."

"So what are we talking? Unrequited stuff?"

"You suffered right along with her," he said.

Ah. Of course, Annie thought. *After all that, it's not so much the love. It's the suffering.*

"I'd do it all over, again, too," she told him. "– Talk about crazy."

The friar took a breath; rubbed the bridge of his nose with thumb and index finger, as if to clear his thoughts.

"Let's grab this picture, he said. "I'll feel better when we're in the van. I'm not like you, I've had enough thrills."

Annie wanted to just give him a nod and keep her mouth shut but her thoughts had a way of spilling out during her more excited moments. "This is where you and I walk across the line, Rafa," she whispered. "– Right at that doorway. You know what I'm saying? No ignoring what we did, no pretending it didn't happen. We leave this room and we're art thieves. Like that Steve McQueen movie – remember? *The Thomas Crown Affair*?" She realized what she was telling him. "*Oh*. No, no, let me rephrase, *I'm* the art thief. Okay? *Me*. You're still my silent partner. Completely silent."

"Wow. You do love this," he said and grinned. "Admit it, c'mon. Before we walk out of the studio, tell me you *love* being the naughty girl."

"I don't dislike it."

"Uh-huh, see."

"Well there's no crime liking something."

"– 'Liking' it isn't the problem."

The Friar opened the door, peeked out, and made an 'ok' sign to Annie. They lifted the painting and walked across hallway, footsteps soft, unhurried. Annie stayed focused on the friar, refusing to look down the darkened hall. When they entered the stairwell, the overhead florescent lights bright on the concrete walls and stairs, Annie had to stop and let her eyes adjust to the light.

"Shit, we're doing this," she said, words breathy.

Fr. Rafa shushed her; told her no celebrating. *Ever*. He told her God's hobby was punishing overconfident thieves.

"OH YOU'RE DEFINITELY being you," Mariel had said. "You *are* the sentimental one." Annie was in the white Econoline, looking at the night and the Calle de Alfonso XII, the street empty except for an occasional passing car. She'd been thinking about Mariel and their Beatles talks – so many talks, and years after the group had ceased to be.

"You okay?" Fr. Rafa said as he watched the road.

"I'm more tired than I thought."

The friar glanced at Annie. "– Are you crying?"

"I'm exhausted. I could sleep for days."

"But you're crying."

She forced a smile. "Surprise. I cry."

"I'm just shocked, that's all."

"I feel ... I don't know –fried." Annie looked out the passenger window. "– Like every neuron in my head is burnt." She stared at her see through reflection. "Mariel and I once did mushrooms together. You know, psilocybin. They're like acid but organic. Like that makes a difference. We thought we were doing something healthy. What can you do, we were kids. So we boiled them and made tea. We tripped for eight long hours. I mean, *long*. When it was done, it felt like my brain had run a triathlon – just like now, just fried."

"We can go to the hospital, if you want."

"No, please. I'm fine."

"The hospital is two minutes away."

"– *No* hospitals."

Annie was looking at Mariel's face in the window – imagining her – the two of them together, see-through faces darkened by the night.

"My sweetheart," Mariel said, her voice gentle and next to Annie's ear. "– You dear romantic, defender of the lost cause. Think you can save that little girl? Is that what you think? Become a thief, be like Steve McQueen? Steal what's not yours to take and keep?"

Annie tried to stop the tremble in her shoulders.

"– Nothing can be done, darling."

Mariel's words scorched very beat of her heart. *Nothing can be done.* Annie shut her eyes tight, not turning from the window, embarrassed by her own emotion, the tears. She raised her hands to hide the sides of her face. This wasn't what she'd ever want Fr. Rafa to see.

18

At the Ritz and Paseo del Prado
Madrid

Taylor decides who to kill first

TAYLOR STOOD ON the hotel room balcony as he talked to Bailey and watched the morning traffic pass by the museum on the Paseo del Prado. The sun was already hot and bright. Across the street the light went through the branches of oak and black poplar in the Plaza De La Lealtad. Taylor had on his UV Ray-Bans and a white terry cloth robe with the Ritz logo on the breast pocket. A cigarette and small glass of orange juice was in one hand, his cell in the other.

Bailey had called him. "How's things going?"

"I can't discuss it on the phone."

"Can I get a generality?"

"– Gone to shit," Taylor said.

"Okay, okay. Clear enough." Bailey paused; then, "Are you *smoking*?"

"I don't smoke."

"Yeah you do. Eddy and I just pretend you don't."

Taylor ignored him. "Eddy is no longer with us."

"– Shit," Bailey said. Then he got quiet.

Bane sat at the glass and wrought iron table near the balcony railing. On the table was a white china plate with what remained of his breakfast – a runny fried egg, a half piece of toast with orange marmalade and an uneaten strip of lean bacon. Beside the plate was today's *Los Angeles Times*, folded and unread, and a snubbed-nose Smith & Wesson M&P 340 magnum. The M&P 340 held five rounds.

"Why are you calling?" Taylor said. He'd removed a box of .357 cartridges from his robe and began inserting shells into the wheel.

"We ... got on each ... other's nerves, Eddy and me." The fat man's voice was very tight and halting, a breathy edge to it. "What the fuck happened, Taylor? What happened to our friend? You and I, we've known Eddy forever."

"This is not a conversation for the phone."

"Hey. Tell me *some*thing."

"The individual we contracted found Eddy's behavior unacceptable. So they parted ways."

"You mean Grendel parted Eddy."

"Why are you calling?" Bane said again, annoyed. He could hear Bailey's shaky little breaths.

"– Bitch killed our friend."

Taylor Bane clicked off his cell and tossed it next to the Times on the glass table.

What the fuck. Who talks about that shit on a phone. Then out loud, "– Goddamn NSA is listening to everything we say, and that fat bastard is going to talk about who killed who and who *should* kill who."

Taylor finished loading the M&P340, aiming the magnum down at a SUV curving about the Plaza De La Lealtad and made a whispered *kapow!* sound and grinned. *Doesn't take much, does it? Just pull the trigger*. He propped his bare feet on the railing, tilting back the red-cushioned wrought iron chair. *Why must I do everything myself? You can't delegate the important shit*. He had no intention of waiting for the Grendel woman to do a job she should've done a week ago. What did it take to put a bullet in Annie Silva's head? A person didn't need a Ph.D.

You aim; you shoot.

Ordinarily Taylor would have stopped payment and had his people go in and beat the rest of the money out of the bitch, the money he'd already given her to do the job. Now the Grendel woman had killed Eddy and the rules had changed. Taylor imagined walking up behind her and putting a gun to the back of her head and telling her, "This is for Eddy." He'd pull the trigger and watch her brains go through her forehead.

No Ph.D. required.

His cell was vibrating on the glass table top. Bailey's number.

"– Yeah," Taylor said, still annoyed with the fat man, waiting for the guy to do another stupid thing.

"It's me. Bailey."

"I got I.D. Why are you calling?"

"I-I apologize."

"*Why* are you calling?" *Christ. How many times.* So Bane said, "Before you start, we won't be discussing the dispute between our associate and the individual we contracted. Is that understood?"

"– Taylor."

"Is that under*stood.*"

"Your interview is in the LA *Times.*"

That stopped Bane in mid-annoyance. Or his annoyance shifted to that a-hole faggot who he hadn't liked from moment one, what's-his-name – *Andreo* Mattos, him and pointy fucking little faggot shoes. *Cocksucking Brylcreemed cunt.* He just could hear Mattos now: "We have a saying in Spain, '*Saber que una persona debe conocer su pasado.*' To know a person is to know his past. Have you heard of it?"

I should've whipped his ass right on the TV.

"– Not all of it," Bailey said, "but, you know, excerpts."

"What're you talking about?" Taylor said, coming out of his bitch-slap fantasy.

"– The *interview.*" The fat man sounded exasperated. "The *Times* is running excerpts. The parts where you don't answer the rape thing."

"*Hey.* Fat boy. I'll tell you what I *do* remember that night. Okay? I remember you looking for your dick. I remember your fat pink gut and you feeling around down there. Okay? Like where's my dick. Like what did I do with my little pink dick."

"... that's not fair," Bailey said, his voice barely audible.

"Don't mess with me this morning."

"I'm answering your *question.*" Bailey sounded lost, not sure what his friend wanted. Or if his friend was still his friend.

"– Attitude, attitude." Taylor was out of his chair, pacing from one end of the balcony to the other, bare feet already feeling the heat of the bricks. "See that's your problem, Bailey – not what you say, *how* you say it. This snotty sarcasm. This 'I'm so much smarter than all you peons, all you peasants.' What sort of man does that to the person who's paying his salary? A pretty fucking excellent salary, I will add. You know what my life is, Bailey? My life is damage control – from the time I get up in the fuckin morning 'til the time I go beddy-bye – damage control. And I'll tell you something, my fat pink-dicked friend –I don't think I can dig us out of this one."

ANNIE LOOKED at a fresh cut across the first joint of her thumb, nothing deep but bad enough to bleed. She was still barefoot, wearing her boxers and sleeveless top from last night – the usual sleeping togs – her dark curly hair uncombed and hiding half her face. Annie had been in the kitchenette holding an apple to the Formica counter with one hand and using a large and very sharp chef's knife with the other. *Not exactly a brilliant idea at eight in the morning.* Now she let warm tap water splash over the cut. The water became pinkish as it washed into the drain of the stainless-steel sink. *God it's good I didn't slice the damn thing off.* Wrapping a paper towel about the cut, she walked toward the bath and bed area, leaving the chef's knife and the quartered apple on the gray and white counter top.

"Tell me I bought Band-Aids."

"You always believed in omens," Mariel said. Another chance to talk with her missed and now imagined companion. Mariel was always there to give support, to answer the unanswerable, a constant muse even in death, especially in death.

"This may not be one of my greatest days."

"See: no Band-Aid and the day's a disaster. Such a Sentimentalist."

"What's so sentimental about that?"

"Haven't you heard?" Mariel voice was wispy, distant. "Pain is your new romance."

Annie found a box of Band-Aids in the teakwood cabinet over the toilet. Two were left and she peeled one open, wiped the cut with Purell, the only antiseptic at the moment, and covered it with the Band-Aid.

"– More prepared that I realized."

"That's my girl," Mariel whispered.

Annie thought it could be a bad day whether she'd cut her finger or not. Liesbet Grendel would be there later in the morning with the girl. *Hopefully, please.* She seemed to want the painting as much as Annie wanted Beth Lee back and safe. But then what? Grendel was being paid to kill Annie, to erase her from planet Earth.

Why would the woman reconsider?

HER EYES WERE vibrating, again. Annie had never once seen Heather when she didn't look crazy. The woman's bleached out blue eyes quivered like a cell with the ringer turned off. Heather Latterimer had come to the apartment unannounced and now stood there with a scary defiance and panic. She had a peculiar sort of beauty but a beauty nonetheless, her long bony legs and arms, her thready blond hair curled and a bit oily. She even had a quarter-sized scab on her right knee. Annie could imagine her getting agitated and tripping on something. Heather Latterimer had the look of a distraught but lovely skeleton preparing for a psychotic break.

Ready when you are, Mr. DeMille.

"– Where is she?"

"How 'bout I get you a glass of wine," Annie said, very calm, nice smile, hoping it all would become contagious.

"Where is *she!*" A screech.

Heather did not walk so much as fling her body in whatever direction she wanted to go. Her high heels clicked across the wood floor. Big leggy gait. Click, click, click. Morning sunshine was coming through the skylights and the floor to ceiling windows, the woman wrapped in its glare. Heather hesitated in front of the covered painting on the new mahogany easel. Annie and Fr. Rafa had placed the painting there last night. Heather was studying the draped white cloth, this odd thing that refused to get out of her way. She seemed bewildered, blinked, then click-clicked around it, heading directly for the large black lacquered divider and the bed area.

"*Baby*?" Her voice was tight, frantic. "Where *are* you, baby? Mommy's Here. No games now."

Annie took a bottle of red from the kitchenette cabinet. *You better get here quick Grendel. Shit. This is going to require drinks, many, many drinks.* She brushed away her dark uncombed hair with a swipe of her hand and poured two glasses of red, leaving the amber bottle on the counter.

Heather had disappeared behind the divider. Annie heard a squeal.

"Where's my *child!*"

"Listen, Heather, let's have –"

"Don't you 'listen, Heather' me!"

The woman appeared from behind the black lacquered divider. Shoulders up, skinny arms stiff by her side, a head first march, click, click, click, toward Annie who held a glass of red in each hand.

Oh God, please no.

I just bought these damn glasses.

She set the glasses on the Formica counter and turned in time to grab Heather's wrists, the woman's sharp cherry red fingernails ready to attack. The woman tripped backward on her heels, boney legs sprawling like a baby deer. Annie scrambling to pin her down, straddling Heather's chest, holding her arms in place. Even pinned, she was trying to strike out.

"– Jesus, Heather."

"– Get *off* me!"

"– Not until you calm down."

"What have you *done* with my daughter?" Heather's shoulders had an irregular quiver, something that would start and stop and start again. There were gulps of air and tears, too, her face lined with mascara cheeks to jaw.

"I have to go to work today. Pay *attention*, please. I can't have Beth with me all day at work. She's six.

She gets bored." *That's the truth*, Annie thought, *or close to it.*

"Did you hit her?" Heather said. There was a break in her shivers, a weird and sudden absence of expression, as though she had just traveled into the center of her own storm. "Did you hit her too hard? Does she have bruises, or –or cuts? It's so easy to lose your temper with –"

"Hey, nobody hurt *any*body." Annie stopped. Something had occurred to her. Then she said, "Do you do that, Heather? Lose your temper?"

Heather shut her eyes. A moment or two later tears began seeping about the edges of her lids. "I think...I...I'm very angry."

Annie was surprised by her own question; more surprised by Heather Latterimer's quick answer. Maybe the woman had been ready to talk but no one was there to do the listening. Annie had felt that way with Mariel, too. She didn't hit her but she would get angry over situations that never mattered until Mariel had become sick – things like not eating, leaving her cloths about the bed, not wanting to bathe, always falling asleep when they were watching the TV together, not wanting to hold or be very close, on and on. Annie had understood but couldn't quit feeling abandoned and angry.

"I'm not a hitter," Annie said, still straddling Heather, pressing her arms to the wood floor. "I yell, though. I'm a big yeller, but that's as bad as it gets. And, no, I didn't yell at Beth."

"– She's a child," Heather said, but to herself.

"Can you stop? Hitting her, I mean."

"Where's my little *girl*." Heather began struggling again. Annie kept a grip on the woman's arms. "– Let's me go."

Annie wanted to ask the question again. *Can you stop hitting your daughter?* She wanted a commitment right there, this second. Maybe Heather's brief confession was all the woman could do now, and she'd escaped into another, safer realm. Some people will get overloaded faster than others. Annie knew this from her time in the hospital years ago, when she thought the Grays hadn't finished with her. Some people are so emotionally swamped they can't move an inch without feeling like shit.

"I have a friend – a very *trusted* friend," Annie said, looking down at Heather.

"She's with Beth. Okay? A very nice woman friend." *Who probably still wants to kill me. But I'm hoping – praying – she won't do that with Beth.* "Are you listening to me? Focus, Heather, Damnit. Stop acting crazy. We could be sitting on the sofa having a nice glass of wine and acting like, you know, human *beings*. Wouldn't you like that?"

"I *don't* drink."

"Okay, fine." *Boy, that's just as well.* Heather drinking wouldn't be a good idea. "You want coffee? I got coffee, tea. I got Sanka. What would you like?"

"Why should I trust you? Who *are* you? The woman had quit shaking but her breathing was a little huffy.

"Fuck, I don't know, Heather. Why did you trust me yesterday?"

"– I-I was scared," she whispered.

"– Of what? Tell me."

"That morning I'd gotten angry. I had to go into the bathroom and lock the door. Beth just didn't want to wear any of her clothes. I know that sounds stupid. When I say it, it sounds stupid. I hate to think of myself like that. Like What's Wrong with the Mother."

"Maybe there's nothing wrong with the mother," Annie said. "I can't tell you the mornings everything in my closet looked like a horror show. It used to drive my dear old father nuts. 'Clothes are clothes,' he'd say. 'Put *some*thing on and get on with your day.'

So I get the closet thing."

"I'd pull one cute little dress after another out of the closet. 'How 'bout this one,' I'd say, and she'd shake her head no. So I'd pull another one out. 'How 'about this one here?' I'd say. It just went on and on. The *child* didn't want to wear anything. It was driving me crazy."

"That's what got you upset?"

"I wasn't like this, you know, before..." Heather let the sentence go.

"– Before the cancer?"

"I guess. Yeah."

Annie relaxed her grip on Heather's arms. "They're going to have breakfast, this woman friend and Beth. They're going for a walk in the park – Jardin Botanico. Maybe go shopping. A decent day, I wish I could go with them." *Especially about now.* Isn't that what you wanted – Beth to have friends? To take a breather?"

Heather shut her eyes. "Please, I don't want my baby hurt."

19

At Annie's Apartment
Madrid

Scenes on Calle Ruiz de Alarcon

TAYLOR BANE SAT in the gray leather backseat of a rented limo, a matching gray curtain drawn over the glass partition between the himself and the driver. This morning he wore his made to measure Savile Row from Alton & Harkey, London. 100% light weight Italian wool, a delicate shadow stripe, roped shoulders, English cuffs, the perfect understated attire for the gentleman who had unpleasant work to do. Beneath the lovely tailored jacket was a holster with his Smith & Wesson M&P 340 magnum, its five rounds already in the wheel. The black limousine had parked across from Annie Silva's apartment building on the Calle Ruiz de Alarcon. Many old trees were spaced evenly along the length of the street. Sunlight shown between the tree branches and spotted the concrete walkway with shadow and light.

"– Keep facing straight ahead," Taylor told the driver.

"We're parked."

Bane retrieved the M&P 340 from its holster, pulled back the gray curtain and the

glass partition. Then he pressed the snub nose of the pistol at the man's head, an inch

below the back of his chauffeur's cap.

"– You a thinking man?" Bane said, very quietly, very polite. "Is that it, a

fuckin' intellectual? All Wittgenstein, Schopenhauer shit?"

"I-I was just saying –"

"Hey, hey. Face. Straight. Ahead. Nod if you understand."

The chauffeur nodded.

Bane shut the glass partition and the curtain. He removed a five-inch titanium suppressor from his jacket pocket and fit it to the barrel of the M&P 340. Placing the pistol on his lap, he leaned back against the leather seat and took an audible breath.

God forbid you should tell these guys something. Bane didn't get it, you pay people and they give you *agita*.

A woman had just walked out of Annie Silva's apartment building. Taylor had

seen her go in twenty minutes ago, maybe a half hour. The woman reminded him of Freddie – very tall, sexy no nonsense walk, nice long legs – but too skinny, no ass. His Freddie had some flesh on her, not fat – *any*thing but fat – but a nice full shape, the sort that other men noticed. He'd always liked that, the way men looked at Freddie. *Look all you want, bud.* Of course if Mr. Romeo got too friendly, the man would learn how much was too much. Taylor also liked that part, establishing boundaries.

The woman's hair looked – he didn't know the exact word – "erratic," was what came to his mind. Even from across the street, he could see her problem: blonde, stringy, curls but not quite curls. Too confusing. Now Freddie had good hair. Thick, red, a nice French twist, no mixed signals, she presented herself well. Classy. This woman across the street needed a cigarette and a Scotch. Maybe a couple of

Scotches. The interesting contrast for Taylor was the woman's clothes. She wore a conservative gray skirt and hip length jacket and a white blouse with a small, prim collar. So you had this contrast, Taylor thought, the conservative clothes vs. her hair, her walk, her twitchy manner, her skin and bones, et cetera. He had her figured, though. The woman wanted to present as if she was very together, very in control, very professional, but all the other parts of her were ready to run screaming through the streets.

The blonde with the confusing hair had stopped walking. She stood beneath a large oak, sunshine going about the leaves and dark branches, the woman bathed in yellow light and tiny fluttering shadows. Taylor watched her, the slender hands rising, the fingertips touching the mouth. Then her skinny shoulders hunched and she squealed, not a long squeal, two or, at most, three seconds. A child was racing toward her, a girl, drifting through sunlight and shade, but a peculiar sort of racing, filled with stops and starts. The girl had on a pale blue cap and she looked even thinner than the woman – the arms, the legs, like bleach twigs in an over-sized pinafore. Running and stopping, running and stopping. The blonde woman squealed again; shouting, *"Baby! Come here, baby!"* Then the blonde dropped to her knees and held out her arms. The girl fell into her embrace and the woman enveloped her, lifting her up, holding her close.

THERE WERE LOSSES, very big losses. Taylor Bane was standing in front of Annie Silva's apartment door. He could not grasp all that he still had – his many years of privilege and fortune – because of what he'd lost this past month alone, and he could not see his own hand in the losing – his political plans, his best friend Eddy, his wife of nineteen years – big losses, all viewed with a rearranging of cause and effect, an ethical and moral amnesia. Bane felt God was conspiring against him. God: twisting in the screws. God: becoming personal and up close. God: throwing him unprepared into a spiritual test equal to Job.

This was when he dove his shoulder into the apartment door.

Wood along the metal hinges splintered. Sections of the door itself flew across the apartment floor. Immediately Bane fired two shots toward Annie who was in the kitchenette having a sip from one of the two previously filled wine glasses. The suppressor on the M&P 340 made a very soft *pop! pop!* sound. But when the .357s hit the cabinets just above her, the wood disintegrated like it had been blow away from the inside with dynamite.

Immediately Annie had ducked behind the tan and red striped corduroy sofa near the kitchenette. She could see the chef's knife on the Formica counter beside the apple she'd quartered an hour or so ago.

"This is long overdue," Taylor said. He wasn't about to just rush over and shoot the bitch. Too humane. Too terror free. No, he always enjoyed letting the person have a moment to reflect on the situation. Stir the juices, so-to-speak. "You know it and I know it – over*due*." His voice had a gentle but impersonal quality, no sense being obnoxious. He was sure his voice had that same respectful tone during their first meeting. Yes, he'd been young. Yes, drinking and other substances were involved. It *was* a party, after all.

But one could go about one's business and still be fucking polite about it. "You and your friend were two extremely hot ladies, I remember that, two beautiful Geishas."

"We were children," Annie whispered.

Taylor fired a third shot, another suppressed *Pop!* This one cut into the top of the sofa and scattered bits of material and cotton stuffing.

"We were all children, bitch."

THERE ARE CHILDREN, then there's you and your demented friends, Annie thought. She laid on her stomach behind the tan and red striped sofa, inching herself toward the kitchenette and the chef's knife atop the counter.

"I was very well respected," she heard Taylor say. "The dean's list, I'll have you know. Straight A student, except for calculus. The best I could do there was a B. One of my friends – you remember the fat boy? Bailey? – he'd just been accepted into Harvard. Just that afternoon, I think. Or a few days either way. Yes, *we* were children, too. We celebrated more than maybe we should have, I can see that. I get your point. Of course you probably don't remember much of anything."

My point? Like it's a fucking debate? Really?

Annie wanted to scream at him, wanted to throw whatever she could grab – *you and your asshole friends raped and tortured us!* – but only a fool provoked a man with a gun, particularly a man like Taylor. Hidden by the sofa, she now leaned against the lower cabinets of the kitchenette. *Or maybe this is the time to provoke him. Shake his ass up.* Annie turned her head; glanced up at the gleaming chef's knife on the gray and white Formica counter top. She was going to put that knife into him. *If the bastard shoots me, he shoots me.* She'd shove the knife into him as deep as she could do it.

"– 'Gentleman songsters off on a spree'," Annie whispered.

"...what?"

"– 'Damned from here to eternity.'"

"What're you saying?"

"AN OLD COLLEGE song," Annie told him.

Taylor knew she was still behind the sofa but he couldn't see her and didn't want to fire the M&P 340. The wheel held five rounds and he didn't need to waste another cartridge. He had extra cartridges but loading them took precious seconds.

"You're an old college boy, aren't you?" she said. "You like the old college boy songs. 'To the tables down at Mory's,' that sort of hokey shit."

"– Not as much as I liked your pussy, darlin'."

"You didn't like my pussy."

"Don't be so sure."

"Oh I'm very sure. I know first-hand, remember?"

"– Be careful," he said, a bit tight.

"That's what this is all about, isn't it?" Annie Silva sounded preoccupied to him. Talking to talk, maybe, but doing or thinking something else ...Taylor didn't know what. She was saying, "I'm a big 'no' to your political wet dream. Congressman, senator – one of those, right?" She didn't wait for his answer; didn't need his answer. "It's like lifting weights, isn't it? For you, I mean. Being a senator or what-have-you, that *power* thing. Ever wanted to lift weights, Taylor? Oh I bet you did. God, I bet that. Weights are for guys who *feel* weak. They don't realize that 'weak' feeling is inside their heads, they got "weak" on the mind. The bigger the muscles the weaker the dude, every woman knows that. Or the smart ones do."

Taylor held the pistol with both hands as he scanned the backrest of the tan and red striped sofa, waiting for some part of her to show, a hand, an arm, something. "So far this amuses me. You're not the cheery sort, but I get it. Hurt feelings, an honest grudge, I blame you not, my dear. I blame you not. Hard for you to believe, I'm sure, but Yours Truly is a sensitive guy. I know–some things can't be forgiven. Yada-yada-yada. No argument from me. I realize I'm not the easiest guy in the world to get along with. You could ask my wife, if she were, you know, *around*."

"What are you saying?" Annie took a breath; murmured, "Where...is she?"

"Don't have a clue. Lost to whim and bad fortune, apparently."

"– Piece of shit."

"Hey, hey. It's okay we're not buddies. Really. I can take it, though I'd advise you to continue disliking me in an *amusing* way. Okay? Are we clear? Are we singing the same hymn here? Pretend you're my Scheherazade and tell Taylor a story. See how long you can keep yourself alive."

Morning sunshine glared through the windows and the skylights and filled the apartment with a yellow-white brilliance. The air was warm and occasionally he needed to squint to see. This was getting less and less of a good time. Taylor decided he could play with her for one more bullet's worth and then he'd have to go over to the sofa and shoot the bitch.

"Tell me a story, Scheherazade," he said.

"You wouldn't like my stories."

"– *Fine*. Jesus." He heard himself losing it, not much, a little, but losing it.

Bane saw her hand reach up and grab a knife off the counter top. *Shit. Where did*

that come from. He fired his fourth shot and missed. The .357 cut into the metal faucet and sent the long thin neck spinning across the room.

"You can come and get me now, asshole," Annie said.

"I'll come and get you when *I'm* ready." He didn't like this attitude, all cocky, all eager to die. But she was behind the goddamn sofa – who knew *where* behind the sofa, exactly – and he had to *know* where – he had to make this last bullet count. Not that he didn't have more cartridges. Of course he had more cartridges. Taylor had a shit pile of cartridges. But he still had the same problem he'd had five minutes ago: did he want to fire the last shot this *moment* and probably miss her and have to reload and waste two, perhaps three seconds, or did he want to wait and get the best shot.

Stupid, cunt. Bringing a knife to a gun –

Annie Silva leaped over the backrest of the sofa, both bare feet landing flat on the cushion. In a single motion she crouched and pushed off, leaping toward Bane with the knife raised. She sunk the blade somewhere between his left shoulder and his chest. He fired his last shot but it was wild, the .357 hitting one of the three kitchenette cabinets and shattering the small wood door. Annie had fallen backward and hit the floor hard. She arched her back and moaned. Taylor didn't know if the bullet had grazed her or what. He began reloading three more cartridges into the M&P 340. The black handle of the chef's knife was stuck in his shoulder, the steel blade about an inch and a half into his flesh.

"– I knew it was you, " A new voice; a known voice. *The Grendel woman.* She was somewhere behind him. "When I saw that black limousine parked by the curb, I said to myself, 'Liesbet, this gentleman's doing his own work.' Am I next on your...what do you call it – your 'To Do' list?"

Immediately Taylor turned and fired. A sliver of the already busted front door spun out into the shadowed hall. But Grendel wasn't there. Now she stood in front of a window, roughly the middle of the room. Taylor didn't understand how she could have gotten from one spot to the other so damn fast. Sunlight surrounded her; reflected off the white cape. The details of her face were lost to the brightness.

"I would've started all this with me," the woman said. "– Not the girl. Always get the difficult ones out of the way right off."

"– Never too late."

Taylor fired the M&P 340 again. The window exploded. Glass spewed from its frame and rained down on the street and sidewalk, some glass scattering across the wood floor.

"I'm right here," Grendel whispered.

Shit. How am I supposed to do this?

Taylor felt her breath on the rim of his left ear. *Shit, please. Tell me how.* Her lips brushed his neck. What came next was a swift, awful pain that sent him to his knees. He didn't know what had caused the pain but ever-so-briefly he had imagined a thick endless needle going through his chest.

"– So quick," Liesbet said.

The woman held the pick by its grooved pearl handle, the grooves fitting each of

her fingers. She had pushed the pick through Taylor Bane's back, between the sixth and seventh ribs and into the edge of his left lung and the left atrium of his heart, the move performed effortlessly. She'd done this before.

Epilogue

Plaza de Santa Ana
Madrid

THEY MET CLOSE to six-thirty, Annie and Fr. Rafa, and sat at their usual table on the plaza. A massive oak shaded them from the last of the day. The evenings were getting cooler now and a pink hue was beginning to thread the sky. Annie had her glass of wine and an order of her favorite tapas, slices of the salt-cured ham. A martini for the friar, of course, his vodka from Girona.

"Are you ever coming back to work?" Rafa said.

"– Tomorrow. I promise."

Taylor Bane's wild shot had caused Annie to fall hard against the wood floor and she'd yanked something in her lower back. Dr. Mora at the Hospital de Madrid said the X-ray hadn't shown any vertebrae damage.

"I've missed you," the friar told her.

"– The same." Annie raised her glass.

"– *Le'chayim*," he said and grinned, touching his glass to hers.

"I'm going to tell them, you know."

"Is that wise?" All expression had left the young friar's face.

"You have no worries, Rafa." Annie placed her hand on his arm; looked at him for a moment before saying, "I don't take away promises and I don't hurt my friends. When it comes to the museum or the policia, it's me and me alone – *not* you and me, not ever."

"I can't let you do that," he said.

"You have no vote." She patted his arm then took another sip of the red. Fr. Rafa was about to discuss who and who did not have a vote on what he did with *his* life, when Annie gave him a friendly Wait-a-Second palms up and said, "Hey listen to this, Heather Latterimer called me last night. We must have talked for two *straight* hours. Seriously, *two* hours. She's really very sweet, you know. A divorced mom taking care of a terribly sick child, she's had it rough. I mean the woman's a little crazy, but *nice* crazy."

"The woman needs therapy," Fr. Rafa said.

"That was part of our talk. She knows."

The waiter glided by with a small round tray balanced on his left hand. He was young, twenties, with shiny parted hair. He wore black pants and a white shirt, his black tie done in a half Windsor and lodged perfectly between the folds of a starched collar. His tray was filled with different types of drinks. He left the friar a second martini and floated on to the next table like a mailman delivering nothing but good news.

"Heather wants to go with me when I talk to the director of the Prado," Annie said. "– Her and Beth. At first I thought that was a terrible idea."

"That's a *wonderful* idea." Rafa was smiling, nodding. "You saved her child's life. What else would any decent, thinking parent do? That certainly could ease our situation."

"– *My* situation.

"We'll see."

"There is no 'we'll see,' Rafa. I'm not that sort of friend."

"You're very dear. But we'll see."

Fr. Rafa would do what he was going to do. He was stubborn the way Big Ben Silva was stubborn. The way Annie was stubborn, too: like father like daughter, she supposed. Whether the friar helped her or not was his choice. She could only tell him what she thought, what she liked and didn't like.

The same was true for Mariel and Beth Lee, when Annie thought about it. Many times you couldn't save yourself let alone other people. Worse, when you believed you saved them, you only saved them for a minute or two. The idea brought her feelings of relief but also helplessness.

"I was afraid Grendel would come back," Annie said. "– If I told anyone why I stole the painting – implicated her."

"You mean she'd remember her contract."

"– A possibility. Who knows."

The friar studied Annie. "You changed your mind."

"The more I thought about it, I knew I was wrong. All Grendel ever wanted was Luc's painting and his diary, that's why she was here. I'm betting sometimes she wanted to burn them, and sometimes she wanted to keep them close. But she *wanted* them. She didn't care about us, what we said or did."

The friar traced the glass rim with his finger. "I've seen nothing about this on the news – no mention of Bane, nothing."

"We won't, I *hope* we won't. I was in and out of consciousness, you know. But I do remember Liesbet bending over me and saying, 'Don't worry, dear. The cleaners are coming.' I didn't know what she meant, not at first. My thinking wasn't very good, God knows." Annie stopped to pick at a thin slice of the salted ham. "Sorry, I'm so starved. Where was I?"

"– Her people were coming."

"Yeah, and they did." Annie finished off the red in her glass and poured herself another from the carafe. "Liesbet called them her 'little family' – an older man and two boys. The boys were like late teens, early twenties, I think. It was *very* surreal. I kept passing out and waking. Then I'd pass out again. But every time I opened my eyes the apartment looked *better* – the front door and the cabinets repaired, the window. I could smell the lilac scent of a disinfectant."

"What about Bane?"

"– Gone. No body, no blood. I mean, *nothing*."

"...wow."

"Oh yeah. The old man even called the ambulance for me."

For a moment Annie and the friar stayed silent. Annie had another slice of the ham and the friar worked on his second martini. The café lights were on now, and the evening had a breeze that once in a while would flutter the leaves of the oak.

"What will happen to Grendel?" Fr. Rafa wanted to know. "What's your best guess?"

"– Probably she'll go back to him. To Luc."

"She can do that?"

"Luc thought so."

Annie still recalled the last page of Luc's diary – though not every word exact, not

every sentence correct. She recalled what had touched her.

But the heart is not logical, is it?

The heart yearns, it feels, it knows its power and leaves all tired and fretting thoughts to the mind.

– Bring back the painting and the diary, dearest, and I will say no more of it. All will be forgotten.

I don't expect you to come to me right away. Let the years pass; let time walk you as slowly as its wishes. You have shown me there are more worlds than this one, and I am waiting for you in mine. I can see it now: I will be out back in the meadow painting and you will appear to me the way you did the first time.

And we will begin again.

ABOUT THE AUTHOR

Ron Savage has published twelve novels and two story collections and a hundred and twenty-five stories worldwide. He has both a BA and MA in psychology and a doctorate in counseling, all from the College of William and Mary. He is a member of PEN America, and has been nominated for the Pushcart Prize and the recipient of the Editor's Circle Award. He has also served as guest fiction editor for Crazyhorse. Ron has worked primarily as a therapist. He has also worked as a newspaper editor, actor and broadcaster.

www.newpulppress.com

www.ingramcontent.com/pod-product-compliance
Lightning Source LLC
Chambersburg PA
CBHW070452260626
47161CB00004B/1274

* 9 7 8 1 9 4 5 7 3 4 2 2 9 *